Spring In My Step
E. Lynn

Contents

Dedication

To my parents, thank you for always teaching me how to work hard and strive for what I want.

And to Zeus, the dog who taught us all unconditional love—and that life can change in an instant.

Chapter One

Kennedy

LAST YEAR'S GRASS WAS beginning to peek out of the melting snow. *It was about damn time.* Moving to Vermont was supposed to be calming and relaxing, but the issue was there was nothing to do. *If I relax any more I may as well lay in a coffin.* Any winter activity seemed too dangerous. *I can hardly walk from one room to another without something silly happening; I either run into something or trip over my own feet.* Therefore, strapping waxed up skis or a snowboard to my feet sounded like a deadly excursion.

I took in a deep breath as the sun heated my cheeks. Holding the fresh air in my lungs, I released it on a long exhale. My eyes drifted to the lilac trees that I was far too excited to see blossom, all that was visible now was the carcases from last spring. A truck's tires crunched as it came up the hill. I lived on a dead end road and there was only one house beyond mine. This mystery neighbor hardly acknowledged me. Making my way to the edge of my property line I waited for the old maroon-rattle-trap to make its way passed.

Like usual I smiled, waved, and got nothing in return.

"Prick," I muttered under my breath when our eyes met. The least he could do was to wave back, give a small smile. The urge to flip him the bird was almost too much as it tingled down my arm to my fingertips.

Cursing the grump, I trudged back into the small house.

It was a cute ranch style house, with an open floor plan. Finally having a space that was all mine had me gushing with the excitement to decorate it. But, it was larger than anticipated and I didn't have enough furniture to fill the space. It echoed back at me as I walked down the halls. It was a bit unsettling. *I need some rugs to muffle that.*

Absent-mindedly picking at a section of peeling wallpaper, I wondered if I'd made a rash mistake. I had more than enough money saved up for the downpayment and was able to find a job quickly after moving. But the problem was that I was lonely. Mel, one of the girls I worked with at the Chiropractor's office, was making my adjustment to the area difficult. Mel had made it a point to ask everyone else in the office out for drinks the last several weekends while ignoring my presence. Childish little... I released a long exhale. The hope of creating a good bond with my coworkers was shot to hell with Mel's terrible attitude.

Smoothing the corner of wallpaper back over the spot it was supposed to be adhered to, I stepped away as it bounced back out.

Maybe I needed a pet. I could get a dog. My parents had never allowed me to have a pet, especially a dog–it might get *hair* on them. I rolled my eyes at the memories of the way my mother's nose curled at the thought of a hairy mongrel running through their pristine house.

And then my stomach clenched in that usual sign of self deprecation.

Squaring my shoulders, I dropped down at my dining table and flipped open my laptop; I needed to get a desk. There was an animal shelter just down the road. I had seen the place while aimlessly driving one day. Another good way to waste time. Pulling up the shelter's website, I scrolled through the dogs. It was astounding the number of dogs the small powder blue building housed.

"Aren't you cute," I said to the screen, at a mutt who looked primarily like a chocolate lab. Clicking through the photos I couldn't suppress a smile. "Alright, Queeny, I think I'd like to meet you." It felt strange talking to a dog on the computer screen—no one was here to hear my new habit of talking to inanimate objects.

I checked the time to make sure they were not yet closed. Fifteen minutes. Grabbing my purse and keys I raced to my car. Determination flowed through me. Maybe I'd be able to find a dog park, meet a fellow dog lover and finally make some friends. I wasn't in the market for a man, but a friend would be good.

***

"Queeny was adopted like a month ago," the teenage girl said behind the counter as she snapped her gum and picked at the imaginary dirt under her midnight-black fingernails.

"Oh," I said, taking in the space. There was a set of curtained glass doors to my right and the exit to my left. "Do you know the last time the website was updated then?"

"Dunno," the girl said, clearly bored. "I'm only here cuz my mom couldn't be."

Not sure if that was meant as the dismissal it felt like, but I pulled my purse higher and turned toward the door, but halted before I pushed it open. I marched back to the counter where the girl stood.

"I would like to see the dogs that are available," I said as assertively as I could, with my back ramrod straight. I'd always been shy and being forceful was not something easily come by. My spine felt strange as did the intensity of my voice.

The girl rolled her eyes and I balled my hands into fists. With an exaggerated huff she pushed herself away from the counter and turned toward the curtained door. She pulled the door open to reveal a long hall with kennels on each side, every kennel had their own doggie door to allow them to go outside. Which I felt was important.

The girl stood and leaned in the doorway.

"Are any of these dogs already claimed?"

She shrugged. "Dunno." If boredom needed a person as reference for the dictionary I was certain I had found the perfect girl for the role.

"Okay," I said, drawing out that end of the word.

Tossing her arm out in the laziest movement to indicate the kennels on the left at the end she said, "Those four came in yesterday, from a kill shelter in some southern state. They're probably available." With her bit finished she turned and presumably headed back to the front desk.

"Great tour," I muttered and walked down the aisle between the chainlink fencing that created the kennel walls and doors. Some of the kennels were empty, one had a large dog that refused to make eye contact and sat in the corner, it broke my heart. He looked so sad. When I crouched down next to his door, the growl he let out without looking at me made me recoil instantly. "Sorry big guy," I whispered as I backed away.

Several of the other kennels along the way were empty. When I reached the last few the girl had indicated I found two small fluffy things, they were quite cute like gigantic cotton balls but I didn't want something I would have to worry a hawk might try to fly off with. Peering into the last two stalls I found a mastiff that looked like he could eat me and a dog that did not have a distinguishable breed. Shifting my gaze between them I hesitantly tried to decide which dog would be best with.

"Hey fellas," I said, kneeling down to better see the mastiff. He had sweet eyes, but he seemed bored, he huffed and flopped down on his standard issue gray bed. "Okay," I said again, dragging it out as I had done before. "How about you?" I said, turning back to look at the mixed breed. Just as I was focusing on him, what looked to be a perfect dalmatian came back in from her doggy door.

I knelt at the edge of her kennel. The dog was gorgeous. All I could think of was the 101 Dalmatians, it hadn't been my favorite movie as a child but I never complained when my sister put the VHS in. Yes, I am old enough to remember watching VHS tapes, 27 wasn't old but it was old enough to remember what many of the new generation had never had to deal with–rewinding a VHS. If there was one thing that felt like it took an eternity it was that. Especially when Kendall had forgotten to rewind the movie when she was done. Kendall either never remembered, or she was too lazy.

A woman in a large bulky black cardigan burst through the door. Her dark curls were haphazardly pinned away for her face and she appeared breathless. "Hi," she said, gulping in air. "I'm Lydia, my daughter told me you were interested in adoption?"

I couldn't hide the way my eyes nearly bugged out of my head at her entrance. "Ah, yeah. I had seen Queeny online and came to ask about her, but your daughter told me she'd already been adopted."

Lydia waved her hand at her flushed face, "Sorry I just finished my Zumba class and Nina hates covering for me here. But that is the only class I've been able to attend so I literally run here from there," she said with a smile and hitched her thumb over her shoulder. I had seen a large brick building behind this one and wondered if it had a gym.

"It's alright," I hedged. Perhaps I should join the Zumba class, it's just dancing right? I mean, how hard could it be?

Lydia nodded, "but yes, Queeny was adopted a few months ago." She grimaced. "I have been working and covering most of the shifts here lately. The last woman that was volunteering moved to Florida last fall. The winters were getting to be too much for her since her husband passed away." Lydia shook her head causing her curls to bounce around her face. "Sorry, too much information. I do that... a lot."

I couldn't swallow the laugh that escaped. It felt good to be able to laugh again. It had been a while. "It's okay."

Lydia seemed to be finally catching her breath. "Alright, so what are we looking for?"

"Honestly, I have no Idea. I have never had a dog and just need a companion. One that likes walks but isn't going to run me into the ground. I am not overly athletic."

Lydia nodded looking around the kennels. "Alright."

That must be her go to word.

"How do you feel about playing fetch? Won't require much work from you other than tossing the ball."

I played softball in high school and the thought of tossing a ball was a welcome thought. I may not have been overly athletic but I could hit something with a bat with pretty good accuracy. We spent a while discussing the available dogs and I was disappointed to find out the dalmatian I had been checking out was already claimed.

Lydia indicated the brown, black and white mixed breed I had been looking at before the dalmatian had entered. "Alright, this little guy came in yesterday from a kill shelter, he looks to be part lab, and some sort of terrier. He is mostly house trained and loves to play fetch from what I've been told. Since you've never had a dog of your own, how would you like to start with fostering? Then if we think it's a good fit for you both we can talk about adoption?"

I knelt by the little guy in question. "What's his name?" I wasn't sure if I should change his name but figured knowing what it was would be a good place to start.

Lydia laughed, "Tito."

"As in the vodka?"

"I think so."

"Do you wanna come home with me, Tito?"

His tail immediately began to wag, I could feel something already bubbling in my middle. *Could it be excitement?* This last year had been a lot, but the thought of having someone at home to see each night brought a bright light to the days ahead. But would I be able to use a dog for happiness? Or would I need to do what I should have done all those months ago?

Go get help, my friends encouraged me. Instead I packed up my life overnight and moved to a new state–probably not far enough away.

Chapter Two

Lincoln

CHECKING THROUGH THE SUPPLY cupboard, I found that I was low on almost everything I needed. How I got myself into this pickle every year I wasn't sure, but here I was again. Sap would be running soon and I didn't have a damned thing for bottling the syrup. Stores would be getting wiped out of all their supplies soon. Creating a mental list, I sifted through each shelf.

But, given the fact that I knew sap would be running soon and I didn't already have supplies lined up… Well apparently I was a glutton for stress.

Closing the last cupboard door I tapped the edge of the metal evaporator, I couldn't wait to see it full again. The first time I came in here and saw sap boiling and moving through the switchbacks, my grandfather had allowed me to boil a hotdog in it all those years ago. I yearned to smell the sap boiling and hear the fire crackling.

Making my way out to my rusting pickup, I knew I needed to replace her but couldn't. So when it was difficult to get it to start I groaned, gave the dash an encouraging pat, and tried again.

On the fourth try she finally revved to life. I would have that checked out. Another item on the list.

Backing out of the drive, I wished my road was paved. The ruts that took their hold on every conceivable inch of this damn road made for the worst driving. No wonder poor Betty didn't want to start, she didn't want to go through the abuse of driving down this jostling road. I would take the unplowed roads of winter over these. They looked like the nasty ribbon candy my grandmother always had around the holidays. If you got a piece that actually tasted good, it would probably slice the roof of your mouth just to be contrary.

Getting down past my new neighbor's house I was surprised to see she was no longer home. She seemed to spend most of her non-working time there. I'd quickly learned her schedule and knew when to predict her car in the drive. She had a two car garage but never parked inside. *Probably a bad driver*, I thought with a scoff.

She always appeared to be wandering around her own property like a lost puppy. She never seemed to know where she should be. Her shotty attempts at yard work had me nearly stopping to help her. But the last thing I wanted was for her to think she was some kind of damsel in distress that I was going to help with everything. I have my own life.

As I reached the end of the road and prepared to drive into town I couldn't help but wonder what she could possibly be doing. It was only five on a Friday night, there wasn't much she could be up to in town.

"Why the hell do you care, Lincoln?" I asked myself as I turned in the direction of town and the hardware store. It was still getting dark earlier than I would like, but the temps were warm this evening. I needed the temp to drop more for the sap to run. This unseasonable warmth may ruin my syrup season.

Getting into the hardware store, I was able to find everything I needed. Thankfully Howard, the man who'd been working in the hardware store since I was a kid, had saved some supplies for me off to the side. Apparently, he'd gotten used to me being a week late to the supply party. It didn't matter what the season was, I couldn't seem to get ahead.

Howard helped me load everything into the bed of Old Betty. Rolling the tonneau cover back into place I was thankful the supplies wouldn't get blown out of the bed of the truck.

"Thanks Howard, how's Mimi doing?" Howard's wife Michelle, had insisted I call her Mimi like all her grandchildren did. I loved the way they'd always accepted me as family, especially after I began living with my grandparents.

Howard's lips pinched. "Cancers spreading."

I didn't–couldn't ask anything more than that. The fact that Howard had still remembered me and my absent mindedness while also caring for his ailing wife made me feel terrible. Howard should be with her, helping her through everything.

"Cammi moved home to help, putting her nursing degree to good use." Howard's attempt at levity sat heavily in my gut. They were the last, almost, family I had. The thought of something now happening to Mimi brought an ache to my chest.

Clearing my throat, I gave the older man a pat on the back that I hoped would convey all that I was feeling, the love of the surrogate family they had become to me. I'd never been the best at relaying feelings; some things didn't get easier with age. I actually felt they became harder. The longer I avoided speaking about my wants and needs the more difficult it became.

Settling in behind the steering wheel, I watched Howard in the rearview mirror as he made his way back into the hardware store. The man had been working himself ragged all his life. He should have been able to retire by now, and he would have if it hadn't been for me. Howard and Mimi should have been some exotic place, living up the best–most relaxing part of their lives. But they couldn't.

The knowledge that it was all my fault had that ball of emotion swelling to an uncomfortable size in my throat. I hadn't allowed anyone to see me cry since the day my grandfather was put in the ground. That was not about to change.

Releasing a pent up breath I turned the key in the ignition. The drive home was filled with the wishes I had for improving Howard and Mimi's situation. There was little I could do. I wasn't some kind of cancer specialist. The time for transplants had passed, there was no way a transplant would be given to an elderly woman who was riddled with cancer in other areas of her body.

So distracted by my thoughts I almost didn't see the woman in the road. It was getting dark and she wasn't wearing anything that would make her presence obvious. Slamming on the brakes, Old Betty groaned to a halt. It was lucky I was already moving slow.

With a groan I rolled down my window, she didn't even move now that my bumper was only a handful of feet away from her. She merely put her hands up in front of her face. Leaning out the window I struggled to temper my tone.

"What in the hell do you think you're doing?"

She leveled me with a glare, her eyes sparkled in the headlights. "Oh ya know, just decided to go stargazing," she deadpanned.

"Get out of the damn road. I could have hit you."

Her small hands balled at her sides, and I was annoyed with how cute it was. "Wow, that is a great idea, I wish I had thought of that," she snapped. And that was when I noticed the entire tops of her boots were covered in mud and there was no conceivable way she'd be able to get out of her current predicament. This was one spot that most of the runoff just happened to end up. Each year it created a mud pit.

"How long have you been there?" I tried–and failed–to keep the amusement out of my tone, and from the glare she sent my way she could hear it too.

"Only a moment before you barreled around the corner."

"Barreled? I was barely going 20 miles an hour."

She harrumphed and bent over to tug on the handle of her boot while trying to lift it out of the mud.

"I don't think.." I started as I opened my truck door. Before I could finish what I was saying, she lost grip of her boot. Then proceeded to fall backward landing on her ass into even more mud with a squelching slurp as if the mud pit were trying to eat her alive.

"Are you kidding me?" she groaned. Assuming it was a rhetorical question I said nothing.

Stepping out of my truck, I stuck to the upper edges of the ruts. Also, I feared I'd start laughing if I tried to speak.

Taking several careful steps to stay out of the sopping pit, I made my way into the lights from the truck. Plunging her into my shadow, she looked so small and vulnerable sitting in the mud. Extending a hand, I helped her to stand. The mud slicked over her palm made it difficult to pull her up, she was petite but the lack of being able to get a good grip was an issue. I didn't want to tug her too hard so it took a moment to get her back into a standing position.

Getting her back on her feet she mumbled a barely audible thanks. A small smile curled my lips as she looked down at her mud covered hands.

I cleared my throat. "You have two options, pull your feet out of your boots and I'll pull them from the mud, or I'll try to help you accomplish what you just tried, but we might end up with the same outcome."

"You expect me to walk through the mud in my socks?" Her dark brown brows furrowed.

Suppressing a groan, I looked down at her feet. "Well you could just stay out here all night until a coyote decides to have you for dinner." I made to turn but there was a tugging on my flannel.

"Okay okay," she says, clearly trying to find the means of escape that would result in her trudging through the least amount of mud.

When she still hadn't made a move to do anything I bent at the waist, wrapping one arm around the back of her thighs and gripping her small yet firm leg.

"What are you doing?" she squealed as I pulled her feet from her boots and began to fireman carry her to the truck. Her hands balled into the material of the flannel on my back. She was going to have this damn shirt coated in mud.

"I don't know if you noticed, but I'm wasting gas sitting here waiting for you to figure out what the hell to do," I said in exasperation. "And as odd as it may be, I do have better things to do with my evening than wait for you." I was being harsh but I hated coming to people's aid. They always expected more in the end.

And I had nothing to give her. She grumbled something that sounded alot like "fucking prick" but I didn't ask her to say it again. Tossing her into the passenger seat I made my way back around to the front of the truck.

Her boots were deeper in the mud than I'd thought. Giving each a good hard tug I pulled them from the sticky muck. The mud this time of year was different than any other time. This turned into something more akin to quicksand. Her boots made a loud slurping sound as they released. Banging them against each other I got as much of the muck off of them as I could, sending small particles of mud all over my denim clad legs.

Climbing back up into the truck, I thrust the boots over to her. She looked grumpy about something. My biting words, manhandling her, or something else, I wasn't sure–but I definitely was not going to ask what kind of bur was up her ass.

Slamming the truck into reverse, I put my hand on her headrest turning to look out the back window while backing down the road. Wispy hairs tickled my fingers. I tried to ignore the feel but something in me itched to wrap my fingers through the strands. To pull her face to mine, to see if she tasted as sweet as she smelled. I couldn't place the fragrance.

Instead, I dropped her off without another word.

Chapter Three

Kennedy

LOOKING AT THE MUDDIED boots by the door, I groaned. It was now Saturday morning and I had finally talked to Mr. Grumpy-neighbor, all because I was literally stuck in the middle of the road. Just thinking about it had heat filling my cheeks. Shaking myself out of my self pitying embarrassment, I needed to get the house set up for Lydia to come inspect so I could move forward with the fostering application. Once I got back home the night before I'd spent the evening watching videos online about building a dog pen. The shelter preferred people to have fenced in yards for their dogs; I'd originally thought about putting a run line up in the backyard. But, a fenced in area was probably best because I could also put in a doggy door and Tito would be able to come and go as he needed.

The thought of the mutt brought a lightness to my chest; something I hadn't had the pleasure of feeling in a long time. I longed to bottle the emotion up and save it for when I needed it most. I could go long periods without the feeling of dread and worthlessness but sometimes it would come over me at the worst possible times. Especially when my father was being particularly unfair.

I wondered for a brief moment if living with me was going to be bad for the furry creature.

"No, Kennedy. Get your head out of your ass," I said, rolling my shoulders back. My heart sank as I looked from the list of supplies I'd made last night to the small sedan sitting in the driveway. I could only hope this small town hardware store delivered. Growing up, my father had stuff delivered whenever he was working on a project; but he always liked to have his space. He never wanted me or Kendall in the way. He always said it was for our safety, but the older I got, the more I doubted that was the case.

Now, I was on my way to a hardware store to pick up tools, lumber and other supplies for something I'd never been taught how to do. I'd been able to find a man online who created videos for people who didn't have fathers, that gave directions and tips on different projects. The worst part was that I have a father, but I have to rely on a stranger like countless others. The videos all had millions of views and thousands of comments thanking the man, so I was comforted to know I wasn't alone.

Walking up to the hardware store, I couldn't help the feeling of being out of place. I hadn't felt so awkward since I was in grade school, knowing everyone was whispering about me. The same feeling spread across my skin now as I stood in the aisle with the power tools. It was an icy fear that caused gooseflesh and sweat to fight for their place as king-of-the-mountain. I was so anxious; it felt as if each person walking by was judging me. Visions of my childhood and leaving my last job played through my mind, people always watching me out of the corner of their eyes. Laughing. *Oh god, am I going to have a panic attack in aisle three next to the damn cordless hammer drills? I don't even know what that means. How can that possibly work?*

"Can I help you find anything?" an elderly gentleman stood at the end of the aisle. There was nothing judgemental about the way he was peering over at me, but there was still that feeling of being stupid that sat in the back of my mind. All the advice I'd gotten from those videos the night before had evaporated from my brain.

"I ah, I need." I pulled the list from my pocket to reference it and break eye contact with him. There was a sadness I could empathize with in him. "I need an eight volt cordless drill." The hammering in my chest only marginally subsided when I found he was giving me an encouraging smile.

"Alright hun." He ambled down the aisle closer to me.

I looked back at the shelf. The tags looked like they were in Japanese. Nothing made sense. Of all the times for me to get into my own head today had to be the worst. The man began to point to different sets and gave me a little bit of information about each.

"Are there any other tools you're planning to buy?"

"Yes, I want a hammer and a few other small tools." I hesitated not wanting to sound foolish. "For ya know, like household stuff." I wasn't sure if I should elaborate that I bought a house and wanted tools just in case. Although, I wasn't sure how I would fix anything if something did happen. *Please don't let anything break.*

The older man chuckled as if sensing my worries. "Don't worry hun; what about this?" He indicated a case that came with the drill, a hammer, a set of wrenches and screwdrivers. "This should be able to take care of most simple things."

I nodded and he took the case from the shelf and placed it in my cart.

"Alright kiddo, what else we got on that list?"

His kindness was easily washing away the anxiety pinching my nerve endings. The feeling of everyone around me judging me and my lack of knowledge about power tools subsided. There were employees helping other people who were likely just as confused as I was–or so I'm going to tell myself

Taking a steadying breath, I pulled the list from my pocket again. "Should I just tell you what I want to build?"

"That would be a good place to start." he peered down at the list, his white bushy brows pulled together in concentration.

"I want to foster a dog, but to do that I need to fence in my backyard. So I want to put up a picket fence and install a doggy door."

"That's great, so you're going to need a post hole digger," he said, raising one of his brows. "I'm guessing since you don't have a drill you don't have one of those."

"No." I laughed. That was the last item on the list.

The older man let out a low chuckle. It was deeper than expected. Everything about him was calm and reserved so his booming laugh caught me off guard.

"Howard?" a man's voice called from the next aisle over.

"Over here," the older man called back shouting over the shelves.

"I thought I heard your..." Mr. Grumpy-neighbor, stood at the end of the aisle. His eyes were darting between me and apparently Howard. Just looking at me had the man's jaw tensing. The annoying part–he was attractive. The dark hair covering his defined bone structure caused my brian to melt a little again.

"Lincoln?" Howard said. I wondered if the older man could sense my attraction and uncomfortability due to his proximity.

"Sorry, I heard you laugh, thought I'd come say hi but I see you've got your hands full."

I narrowed my eyes. I wasn't sure if this was an insult or not. Granted the man had saved me and my boots from the middle of the road.

"Yes, I'm helping, I'm sorry hun I didn't catch your name."

"Kennedy," I smiled over at Howard.

"Kennedy," the older man repeated looking to, well now I supposed his name could be changed to Grumpy-Lincoln.

"We've met." He said it like it was something disgusting to admit.

Howard looked between us again. The man may be old but he knew there was more Lincoln wasn't saying.

"I don't know if it counts when all the Grump does is yell at you."

Lincoln practically growled, "she bought the Anderson's old place."

"Ahhh, so you're neighbors. That's great."

"How do you figure?" Lincoln asked, letting his doubt seep into the question.

"Not the way I see it," I mumbled under my breath, our words overlapping one another and Howard let out another booming laugh.

"You'll get used to him hun," Howard said to me. It did little to reassure me.

Lincoln rocked back and forth as a smirk spread his lips. "Nice shoes, going for any walks today? Should I get my tow chains ready?"

"You wouldn't be able to tow sh–"

"Alright dear, what's on your list again?" Howard cut me off, clearly knowing whatever was going to come out next was not going to be overly neighborly–if at all.

With one last glare at Lincoln I read off what I thought I was going to need. I'd found a quilting ruler in one of the totes in my basement. It wasn't the most accurate way to measure something and I'd been thankful Lincoln hadn't driven by while I was out there flipping it end over end in the mud and snow to get an estimate for what size fence I'd need. The ruler was three-feet long.

"What the hell are you building?"

"Why the *hell* do you care?"

"Alright kids. Lincoln, why don't you go out and see if you can find Stimpy? Let him know I'll be out soon and I need some lumber cut."

Lincoln's jaw shifted but without another word he stalked out of the aisle. I was embarrassed and annoyed with myself for allowing my eyes to peruse his backside. It was chilly out this morning and he'd donned a navy and forest-green flannel; the dark wash jeans did more for him than I wished to acknowledge. Finding this man attractive despite the irritation directed at him was galling.

"Did you just call someone Stimpy?"

Howard chuckled. "Yeah, it's a nickname. He came here almost a year ago and I still have no idea where the name came from."

I allowed a smile to crest my lips. I may find my neighbor beyond rude, but he at least had somewhat good taste in friends. I narrowed my eyes in Howard's direction. Or were they family? It was possible.

"He's not as bad as he seems, I promise."

I shrugged off his comment. Seven years was how long I'd spent in my rental near my father. And in those seven years I never spoke to one of my neighbors. That feat could be surpassed. Lincoln wasn't someone I needed.

"Follow me this way and we'll find you that post hole digger. Have you ever used one?"

"No but I did watch some videos online. I think I have a good idea of how to do it."

One of Howard's fuzzy brows shot up. "You got family 'round?"

"Not really, my father is about three hours away in Manchester, New Hampshire."

"You traded city living for this?"

Although I walked slightly behind him as he wove through the aisles, I knew there was a smile on his face. After finding what we were looking for I handed over my small list of lumber needs; Howard scanned it and the amateur drawing I'd included.

Howard did some calculations and helped determine what was needed. When we made our way to the register Lincoln came up behind us.

"Stimpy is ready," Lincoln said, the annoyed tick still in his hard set jaw. The stubble on his cheek called to me to rub my hand over it. I wanted to feel the way it would prick against the soft flesh of my palm. Those thoughts were dislodged with a strong shake of my head.

"I have a few things I need to pick up for sugaring that I forgot yesterday. I'll see you later Howard, give my best to Mimi."

"Not so fast, son." Howard latched onto the shoulder of Lincoln's flannel.

Lincoln stopped and lifted a brow at Howard. I tried to keep my nose out of whatever they were talking about, but they were so close and Howard wasn't done helping me. It was far too easy to track their movements and conversation out of the corner of my eye.

"You're going to need to bring Kennedy's lumber home for her."

I nearly dropped the box of screws I was about to place on the belt.

"Jamie called out, we don't have a delivery truck driver."

"Fuck," Lincoln muttered and I couldn't suppress that feeling of being a burden.

I didn't need these feelings, again. Not from him.

Chapter Four

Lincoln

"No, no. That's okay. I can, ah," Kennedy rubbed her forehead and looked around as if someone with a magic carpet was going to be flying in to bring her lumber home. "I can put the project off until he's back at work." Her cheeks flushed either at her rambling or the realization that we all knew she was clearly listening to our conversation. We were a mere three feet away from her, but still, it was obvious she'd been listening to us.

"I thought you wanted to get that dog soon?" Howard asked.

The confusion on my face as I looked over to her had her cheeks turning a deeper shade of scarlet. The urge to mock her for eavesdropping itched to drop from my lips but I knew it would likely end with a smack upside the head if Howard overheard. The man was like another grandfather, and he took the role seriously, since he didn't put up with any of my crap, no matter who it was directed at. Especially if Howard didn't think they deserved the mockery.

Suppressing a groan I said, "I drive past your house to get home. It will be fine." Really, I wanted to ask about the dog but was not going to allow myself to get pulled in by her.

Shrugging she turned back around and began loading up the belt with the last of the smaller items in her cart. The cashier came around the counter to scan the shovel and post hole digger. The way Kennedy ignored me set off something indignant I couldn't stop. "What, you can't just take your dog for walks like most people?" As I said it I sidestepped Howard to make sure there was too much space between us for him to reach me. However, that didn't stop Howard's glare.

Kennedy balled her small fists at her side. "Not that it's any of your business, but it's a requirement from the shelter."

"Anything else?" Cherice asked from behind the counter again. Perhaps trying to distract and diffuse my building anger.

"Yes," Howard said, stepping forward and giving me one more warning glance. He told the cashier all the lumber that would be needed and asked her to ring it up. Kennedy stood at his elbow. She looked over her shoulder, I could only assume it was to look at me.

Why did she have to move into that house?

"Keys!" Howard barked. I knew I'd lost. I tossed the keys over to Howard. He snatched them out of the air with the agility and precision of a ninja. Another moment to show me that old age doesn't mean decrepit.

"What'd ya do to him?" Cherice asked, ringing through the last few supplies I needed.

I shrugged. The image of Kennedy standing in the sticky mud flashed in my mind.

"Have a good one Cher," I said as I took the small plastic bag from her. Her cheeks flushed and I could have kicked myself for forgetting she had a crush on me. It made going into the hardware store almost painful. She was two years younger than me and had made everyone aware that she liked me and would one day want to be my wife. I wasn't sure if this declaration was to ward off other women, but it was not one that I wanted to be followed by.

Exiting the store, I nodded to some of the locals as I made my way around the building to find my truck. Kennedy was standing by the bed of the truck wringing her hands as the lumber was loaded in. My shoes crunched on the asphalt as I made my way to them but, over the sound of the saw, no one else heard my approach.

"I just don't know why he hates me so much," Kennedy said to Howard, her back to me. There was a sharp pang of guilt in my stomach.

"Give him time."

"Give who time?" I interrupted, taking a little too much pleasure in the way Kennedy's eyes opened wider than usual. It gave her the look of a cartoon character whose eyes would shoot out of their head in surprise.

She recovered quickly though. "Eavesdrop much?"

To stifle a smirk I had to flex my jaw. The motion made me look more pissed off than usual and was a good go-to when I didn't want to be bothered. Instead of being deterred she seemed to be spurred on.

Her eyes narrowed. "Howard was just telling me how you'd love to help me get all these posts into the ground. That you're such a *nice guy*," she said using those stupid air quotes, "he saw no reason why you'd say no." There was the glint of a challenge in her eyes.

Howard looked perplexed at first, but then a slow smile curled his wrinkled face. I pressed my tongue to the side of my mouth, and took a step closer to Kennedy. I don't know why, but for some reason I wanted to be in her space, call her bluff.

As I stepped closer I caught that fragrance again. Something floral, I wished I could place it, I wanted to come up with something smart to say to her. But the opportunity was squashed when Stimpy loudly announced all the lumber was ready.

Before moving around Kennedy, I didn't miss the way her breathing had increased when I'd been but inches from her. Something had flickered in her eyes. It almost looked like fear. I shook my head as I pushed Howard away from the pile of prefab pickets and the rails, which had been cut down to size.

"You're going to help her, right?" Howard asked and I didn't miss the note of expectation in his voice, and the threat of a verbal lashing if I begged off.

"We'll see."

Howard grinned knowing that was as close to a yes as he was going to get. If I didn't care for the man so much I would have refused, and he knew it. There was something about this woman that intrigued me and also immediately rubbed me the wrong way. It was likely the way she just seemed to always get herself into trouble. And by always I meant the night before, because I had seen her gardening and doing other yard work in the fall with no issues. Clumsily for sure, but without problem–or injury. It wasn't her. It was the tug I felt anytime I saw her. The way she always seemed to look lost and I wanted to be her compass that would lead her home.

I'd tried to be that for someone once before. Not going to go there again.

When I spun back around to get into my truck, I nearly collided with the woman who was using the space in my brain as a lounge area. The fence that *should* be erected needed to be between my emotions and anything that had to do with Kennedy.

She opened her mouth to deliver what I assumed was going to be a scathing remark about knocking into her, but she quickly shut her mouth again. I let a cool smirk cross my face as I lifted one brow. I was about to do her a favor and I hoped it would help to keep her from acting like a brat, or at least quiet.

Breaking eye contact, it looked as if she was examining a button on my flannel; a different one than the one she smeared mud all over the night before. A frown pulled her brows together and I wanted to wipe the wrinkle that formed off her forehead. She was nearly a foot shorter than me, the top of her head barely reaching my shoulder.

"Thanks," she muttered to that spot on my chest.

"I'm sorry, what was that?" I asked squatting slighting to bring our eyes level. I knew it was a condescending move, and I will fully admit it was to get her riled, but I couldn't help it.

With a grunt she repeated, "Thanks," with far more sass and much louder than the first time.

I pat her on the top of the head. "Happy to help, Piglet," I said in my most mockingly sweet voice.

"Excuse me?"

"Well I figured you liked to play in the mud, since you oh so kindly covered both me and the seat of my truck in it last night. So the cute nickname seemed appropriate."

The faintest trace of a grimace flashed across her face. "I'm surprised you were able to notice anything different."

And with that she spun around, her auburn hair fanning out behind her. My eyes fell to watch the swish of her hips and ass as she walked away. So, she liked to get the last word. I would make sure it was a little more difficult for her from here on out.

Sliding into the driver's seat, I waited while she climbed into her car. She adjusted the radio, messed with her phone, and then finally got buckled. At this rate I was going to get to her house just before dinner. Looking down into her car I felt a bit guilty for virtually spying on her but we were in a public parking lot. Was it really as creepy as it felt?

Shaking my head, I started the truck trying to give her a not so subtle hint that I was ready to go. Obviously I knew where she lived but I didn't want to park outside her house and wait for her. She started her car and hesitated with her hand over the shifter.

"What the fuck are you doing now?" I groaned.

Pressing something on a laptop sized screen on her dash she began talking. Fantastic, now I had to wait for her to make a phone call.

Leaning out my window I brought myself as close as I could to her passenger window without actually removing my entire body from the truck. Her body started to shake, *was she having a seizure?* I moved for the door handle and realized it was worse. She was crying. Whoever called her upset her and I was not a man who did well when a woman cried. Hell, I didn't do well when anyone cried. Child, man, woman, it didn't matter. The moment the waterworks started I wanted to run.

Trying to move myself back into the truck as quickly as possible my hand slipped on the edge of the window, and I dropped onto my ribcage. Releasing what would likely be equated to the sound of a whoopee cushion landing on the ground after being dropped off the top of the Empire State Building. And she was looking at me.

Tears glistened in her eyes, and I'd just knocked the wind out of myself, half dangling out of the truck window and was currently wheezing. It was worse than when Tim at the deli got into a coughing fit; the man had been known to smoke nearly two packs a day. And when he started hacking, it was bound to last more than five minutes.

The window at my face rolled down. She sniffled but lifted her chin. "So you *do* make a habit of eavesdropping." With a glare, she shifted, and was peeling out of the parking lot before I could finish catching my breath.

"Shit," I muttered. I didn't want to ask her what was wrong but the drive to her place would only take five minutes. I hoped she would be better by then and that I would be able to explain that I wasn't trying to listen in on whoever she was talking to.

Maybe it was an ex, I didn't like that thought. What if it was a current boyfriend? I liked that idea even less. I didn't want her but I also didn't want anyone else to have her. Well, I wouldn't allow myself to think about having her was more the accurate way to put it. She was far better off without me fucking up her life. She could ask nearly anyone in town. They'd say the same. Except maybe Cherice, I thought with a shiver.

Chapter Five

Kennedy

As if an argument with my father wasn't enough, Lincoln heard it. If he didn't hear it he'd no doubt seen me crying. Fan-fucking-tastic. I'd seen him scrambling away from my car and smashing his ribs off his window. The humor of it actually helped stop my crying.

Releasing a slow steady breath I backed into my driveway; shaking the tension out of my shoulders I tried to focus on what needed to be done. This would be one day–hopefully only one day–of working with him. Then I could go back to normal life. But now I wouldn't bother wasting my time waving to him. Knowing the prick he was, I didn't see any reason to continue trying to have any sort of tentative friendship. If it could even be called that. But even as the thoughts swirled I felt guilty.

Shifting my car into park, I waited as Lincoln backed in next to me. Once his truck stopped he sat as stiff as a statue staring straight ahead.

Sighing, I exited my car and rounded the front until I was standing at his driver's side door. I tapped a single finger on the glass. The sound must have snapped him out of whatever strange haze he was in because, for a moment, he looked startled to see me; then he shook his head sending his dark hair flapping around his face.

He quirked a brow and that was when I realized I had a stupid grin on my face. How did I go from despising him to thinking... oh god, was I thinking he was attractive. Nope, nope that was not possible. I did my best to tamp down the smile but likely made myself look insane instead.

"Are you really getting a dog?"

Startled by his abrupt, snappy question, the smile now easily slid from my face, splatting onto the crushed stones beneath my sneakers.

"Yes," I crossed my arms.

"Why?"

"Clearly because I want one," I snapped.

"Have you ever had a dog?"

"I don't owe you a Q&A session."

"You kind of do since I am giving up my Saturday to build you a damn fence," he said with a glower.

Suppressing the urge to stomp my foot I replied through gritted teeth, "no, I haven't."

"Great, so what's going to happen when this new *fad*" mimicking the quotes I'd used on him earlier. "Loses its initial luster?"

"I don't think committing to a dog is a *fad*." I mimicked him in return, wanting to shove the word down his throat. "Plus, I have to foster before they will actually let me adopt." I kicked at a few of the stones beneath my feet, worried I would botch this opportunity. If I hadn't had the argument with my father this morning I would be able to think more clearly and argue better but, with my father's cruel words and now Lincoln's clear doubt in me, I couldn't help the feeling of being inadequate.

"So you're spending how much just for a trial period?"

"You know what, you can fuck off if you want to give me a hard time about everything I do. I will figure this out on my own. I don't need you or anyone else," I snapped. The stones crunched angrily under my rough foot falls. I made my way around the truck and dropped the tailgate so I could begin to pull the lumber from the back. "I'll get my shit out of your truck then you can go."

Lincoln chuckled then sighed and ran a hand down his face. "Fuck me," he said on a groan. "I'm sorry, I'm not good with people all the time."

I scoffed. "How about ever? You have been a jerk to me the moment I got here–the first time I spoke to you." I glared at him. Dropping my gaze then said in a whisper, "and I don't deserve it."

Focusing on my hands, I pulled a post from the bed of the truck and began a pile on the edge of the garage. If I wanted to get this done this weekend I didn't have time to play games with Lincoln.

When I made my way back to the truck to get another post my path was blocked.

"I know you don't want to be here so please let me just empty the truck so you can go." I kept my eyes trained on anything but the deep blue eyes of the man in front of me. I zeroed in on an ant making its way across the drive. It seemed to stumble over each rock–*me too little guy*.

One calloused finger tipped my chin up so I was forced to look into his eyes. "It's not that I don't want to help," he said and then tipped his head from side to side as if deciding on the best way to say it "I'm just shit at making new friends."

"That sounds like an understatement," I grumbled.

He let out a gruff laugh, when his hand dropped from my chin I felt a loss at the absence of his touch.

"I will try to do better."

I nodded, I needed to keep some distance between us. I was vulnerable right now and wanted someone's attention–or approval–would be the more accurate way of saying it. My *daddy issues* needed to remain just that, *mine*. The last thing I needed was to allow myself to get caught up in another person. Especially this man.

Lincoln draped his flannel over the side of the truck bed to reveal a white cotton undershirt and far too many muscles. My middle tightened at the revelation. He just moved five notches up the hot-o-meter which meant I needed to add at least five feet to the distance between us. At. All. Times.

Deciding he had the removal of the lumber under control, I scurried over to my car and removed the other supplies from the trunk. With my head stuffed in the trunk I took a few calming breaths, reminding myself that under all that muscle Lincoln was an ass.

"What are you doing?"

I yelped, jumped, and hit my head off the inside of the trunk. I'd managed to hit my head on the light. Rubbing the spot, a welt began to form before I could come up with a good excuse to be virtually inside the trunk.

"I was just getting the other supplies."

Lincoln's brow quirked. When I looked back down I realized everything had rolled to the edge, directly in front of the opening. *Smooth, Kennedy, real smooth.*

"Right," he said, dragging the word out and letting the word linger. Then he shook his head and made quick work of the remaining items in the bed of the truck while I removed my new tools and ran inside to make myself a cup of coffee. Two a day was my limit. Usually.

"Do you want a coffee," I asked, sticking my head out the front door.

He shook his head, "A water would be nice," and then, as an afterthought, he rushed to add "please."

I nodded and went back into the house. Grabbing bottled water from the bottom drawer of the fridge I returned outside, with my coffee in the other hand. The morning sun was quickly melting the thinner patches of snow.

"Where do you want it?" he asked leaning on the tailgate of his truck.

"Well I was thinking I want to include the front door, so it's easy for him to go out. Then go out to the end of the garage and follow the length of the house and meet back at that corner." I pointed to the far side of the house.

Lincoln nodded. He pulled a small note pad from his back pocket and a pencil from behind his ear. I hadn't noticed it there before. Furrowing my brow I tried to recall if it had been there at the hardware store. No, I was nearly certain that it hadn't.

"Hello?" Lincoln called, waving his hand in front of my face.

"Huh?"

"I asked you where in the fence you wanted the door? Near the garage for easy access to the driveway or in the middle so it looks symmetrical?"

"Oh." I hadn't given much thought to where the door would be placed, I'd just assumed it would go near the garage, but now that I tried to picture it, it would look better centered. "Centered? It likely won't be used most of the time anyway."

Lincoln nodded and made a few notes on his pad. He opened his mouth and then slammed it shut again.

"Trying not to insult me?" I raised a brow assessing him.

Lincoln smirked. "Something like that"

Between the smirk, muscles, and the shirt I didn't know how I was going to convince my body that I was not attracted to this man. Feeling awkward, I stayed just to Lincoln's right and watched as he sketched out his plan for the fence. Twice he'd measured the distance from the garage to the corner of the house and then from the house to the corner of the garage.

His penmanship was nearly impossible to read at this distance. I couldn't tell if it was sloppy or just really small. Either way I didn't want to get any closer. He tucked the pencil back behind his ear, which I was beginning to find endearing, and he went back to his truck. As he dug around in the backseat, I felt a bit out of place. I clutched the coffee mug to my chest, it was no longer steeping hot, but was lukewarm. I nursed it as long as possible.

For some reason my anxiety decided today was the day. The day it would make me feel awkward in my own skin; everything I did felt strange. A man who didn't like me, was almost bullied into helping build a dog fence. He had hardly spoken to me since I came back outside and I didn't know what to do with myself. *Should I follow him, ask what he was doing? Stay in this exact same spot for the entirety of the day?* Neither option seemed particularly appealing, but I stayed right where I'd been since coming back out with my coffee. I wanted, more than anything, to feel useful.

Sighing, I tapped my nails on the ceramic then downed the last of the coffee.

Turning on my heel I went back to the house. Even walking through the house I felt like an imposter. What was I doing here? Would I really be able to make a life for myself? Or was my father right? Was I destined to screw this up like I did most everything else in my life?

I shook my head, I would not be letting those tears reappear. The man who brought me into this world didn't deserve this much stock to be put into his words. Heat filled the back of my eyes and my vision began to blur.

"Kennedy?"

I cleared my throat trying to push back the tears begging to be released. "Yeah?" I asked, trying and failing to make my voice sound normal.

A long pause followed.

"I ah, I thought I had spray paint in my truck, but I don't. I'm going to run up to my house to get it."

"Okay," I choked out.

Another long pause, I didn't hear the tell-tale squeal of the door, so I knew he was still in the house. His footsteps echoed as he rounded the corner peering into the kitchen.

"Are ah, you alright?"

"Yeah, fine."

"I really am sorry for being a dick earlier." He rubbed his hand across the back of his neck avoiding eye contact.

"We only have to tolerate one another for today, right?" I asked with faux brightness. "I'm sure we'll survive."

I was surprised to see hurt in his eyes when he looked up at me. There was something sad about him. "Right," he snapped, turning on his heel and slamming the door on his way out.

Great.

Chapter Six

Lincoln

How was this woman getting under my skin so easily? I only started speaking to her yesterday and already I wanted to run as far from her as I could. Self preservation ran strong and it was nearly too much to contain. There was something wounded about her that wanted to pull my damaged soul to hers. *So what? Then we could compare their scars? Heal?*

I shook my head as I drove back down to Kennedy's house after locating the neon orange paint in my garage. I'd used it a few years ago to mark the trees I needed dropped on my property. I hoped it was still good.

Something about a crying woman caused me to choke on the air attempting to permeate my lungs. I hated it. Likely because that was all my grandmother did in the last few years of her life. She cried during every holiday and even the moments that should have been happy ones. I'd always done everything I could to make her happy. Nothing worked. My grandfather had told me on numerous occasions that it was not my fault, that she had more going on that I would likely ever know.

I tried to shake the image of seeing Kennedy crying and almost crying. Once I knew nothing was my fault, at least I hoped, the second time I couldn't be too sure. Part of me itched to figure out what was wrong and try to fix it for her. But that usually led women into thinking I wanted more from them. The last thing I was looking for at the moment was a relationship, especially not with someone who may be as fucked up as me.

I'm a hypocrite.

Pulling back into her driveway, I was surprised to find her outside again. She had unbundled some of the pickets and was lining them up so they would be ready to be attached to the rails and then to the posts. She had selected the scalloped pattern which would look nice painted white against the navy blue of her house.

As I hopped out of the truck, she stood to face me & rubbed one hand up and down the opposite arm-looking troubled. If a look could be attached to an alarm it would be that one, telling me to run, run, run. Lights should also be flashing in her eyes signaling that something disastrous was to come.

"About earlier," she said hesitantly. "I didn't mean to offend you, I'm having a bit of an off day."

"You didn't offend me," I said with my brows pulled together.

"Oh." her eyes left mine, making me feel the loss. "When I said we only needed to tolerate one another for today you seemed... angry."

My gut clenched at her repeating the words, "Nope, all good." I tossed the spray can in the air, catching it in one hand. "Ready to build a fence?"

Her shoulders relaxed. "Yup. I watched a ton of videos last night on how to build a fence so this should be pretty easy."

I had to force myself not to cringe. Great, an internet educated expert.

Taking out the tape measure I began to cross reference the distances to mark out where each of the posts needed to go as well as where the gate should be, to center it on the fence. Kennedy followed me asking questions and reminding me of an over excited puppy. A dog might be good for her. Maybe it will even match her energy. I chuckled and shook my head as I tossed the paint back into my truck.

"What's funny?" she asked from behind me.

She was so close it felt like she was nearly on top of me it made me jump and my heart race. "Fuck," I muttered as I turned to find her standing just by the edge of my truck door.

"What's wrong? Did I scare you?" She smirked as she teetered back and forth, this was a far more chipper version of the woman I'd seen only an hour ago. And I'd be lying if I said I didn't like this happy joking version better than the sad doe eyed one who'd looked on the verge of tears.

"I think if I snuck up on you and then shouted into your ear you'd jump too."

"What? I didn't shout. I spoke at normal volume and I certainly didn't sneak. That's a bit hard to do on this driveway."

She kicked at the stones, sending a few skittering closer to the road.

She was right but I was not going to concede. Instead I tipped my chin in the direction of the post hole digger. "So, Construction Queen, show me what you've learned."

Her eyes lit up like I'd told her she could open the first Christmas present of the morning. She nearly skipped over to the tool, taking it in hand and positioning herself over the first orange 'x' I'd made.

"Whoa whoa whoa, first off, did you get any work gloves?"

She shook her head slowly, I sighed and leaned back into the truck. Lifting the back seat I found a pair of work gloves, they would be several sizes too big, but hopefully they would prevent her hands from blistering. After dropping the seat back down I noticed my radio on the other half of the bench seat. Lugging it out with me, I set it up while Kennedy put on the gloves.

"I look ridiculous," she grumbled as she frowned at the offending yellow gloves. She bent the tip of one of the glove fingers over to show they were at least an inch too long on each finger.

"You don't want to use that thing without gloves on."

The longing in her eyes told me she really wanted to try out her new tool. I'd never seen a woman want to try using a post hole digger so badly. "Fine, I can make these work." she tightened the velcro around her wrist, as tight as they would go, they still looked loose but I wasn't going to mention it.

"Country?" She looked at me as if I were some sort of traitor.

"Who doesn't like Morgan Wallen?"

She pointed at herself with the too large gloves and I feigned hurt, holding my heart.

Kennedy rolled her eyes and positioned herself over the first 'x'. I couldn't suppress the laugh when she tried to force the ends into the ground with the handles pulled apart effectively making her attempt useless. Assuming she didn't hear me, I watched as again she slammed the metal into the ground. From my vantage point she made little to no headway. Her brows furrowed as she scowled down at the ground. The urge to use my thumb to erase that damn line of confusion between her brows had my legs begging me forward. As if I were a puppet and something in her held the other end of those damned strings.

"Why isn't this working?" She stomped her foot.

"You ah, need to open the pincers."

"What?"

"Push the handles together and try again."

She rolled her shoulders and prepared for another attack. This time with the pincers perpendicular to the ground she made it down a few inches. She grinned up at me and another tug from the puppeteer had me pushing off the tailgate.

The smile tilting up my lips was impossible to resist. "Perfect, now try to do that a few more times, make a circle like a perforation and then you will be able to start pulling dirt out."

Beaming, she nodded and went back to work.

The spring sun was beating down on us. I used my flannel for at least the tenth time as a sweat rag. Kennedy impressed me by digging three of the eight holes needed. Now she was ever so carefully screwing the pickets into the rails. She was meticulous with each one ensuring it had the same distance between both the top and the bottom before screwing it in. I only had to show her how to use the drill twice before she caught on. Perhaps her YouTube education hadn't been an entire waste of time.

Forcing the post hole digger into the ground, I paused to watch her. Twice she measured and then shifted the picket before screwing it into place and then repeated the same double measurement on the other end.

"You sure you've never done something like this before?"

"Positive," she laughed. "I think this would be the last thing my father would want me doing."

I quirked a brow.

"Manual labor that is."

It was not the response I was expecting; I made quick work of digging the last two holes. I was beginning to get more and more curious about this woman. She didn't seem to have many friends, not here anyway. Someone had enough hold over her emotions to render her into tears in the span of a less than two minute conversation. Her father didn't believe she should be doing manual labor.

I never gave much thought to having kids, not because I didn't want them, but because I couldn't see myself finding a woman who I'd want to settle down with. But when I did picture my kids I always pictured a boy and a girl. They would help me with sugaring and they would spend summer evenings outside playing yard games. Going for hikes and getting dirty. Those were the things I did as a child, and most of my friends, but as I watched the sensitive yet sassy woman across the yard I knew she had a vastly different upbringing. Hell, she'd never used a power tool until today. And the prospect of doing so had brought her such excitement.

I wondered what her past had been like and what caused her to buy the house down the road from me. My mind was going places I didn't want it to. This was a one day thing—us working together. Tomorrow would be back to normal. I wouldn't be spending evenings with this woman getting to know her and all her quirks. So, I needed to get all the nosey thoughts out of my mind and get back to the task at hand.

"Holes and posts are in," I said as she used the neck of her tee to wipe her forehead, revealing a sliver of tanned, toned skin just above the waistband of her jeans. Fuck. If my mind was already thinking things it shouldn't it just got a million times worse. Now the thoughts of how soft that skin would be burst into the forefront of my mind.

"Earth to Lincoln," Kennedy said waving her work gloves in the air as if she was waving someone down for help.

"What's up?"

She frowned, "I asked if you were ready to break for lunch, it's already half past noon." She tipped her head to the side, much like a dog would. I needed to stop comparing her to animals. Although that was the reason we were out in the early spring heat building this fence.

"Sure, what did you have in mind?"

"I can run down to the store and get us sandwiches."

"Alright, sounds good to me. I can give you cash." I made to head for my truck.

She shook her head, "No, please, let me do this for you as a thank you. I really do appreciate all your help. And I'm sorry for this morning. I was having a tough time."

I didn't want to hear her apologize anymore.

"It's done, let's just try to be friends."

"Just for today?"

I chuckled, "We'll have to wait and see how the rest of the day goes. Then I'll let you know. I have a serious vetting process."

She scoffed and rolled her eyes, "I bet."

In a way it was true; since my parents' deaths I did my best to keep most people at arm's length. I was beginning to realize it was not going to be easy to do that with her.

And that made me nervous.

Chapter Seven

Kennedy

CLIMBING INTO BED THAT night, I found I hurt in places I didn't even know had muscles. I felt great until the moment we stopped working. Once the tools were put away and I sat down for the first time all day I discovered how painful manual labor could be. To say I had a sheltered childhood would be a vast understatement.

My father was a man who wanted his daughters to be nothing more than something pretty to be brought out during special occasions. Refusing to let him take up space in my mind, I opened my phone to find a text from an unknown number. Butterflies came to life in her middle.

Unknown Number: See you tomorrow–Lincoln

Three words and I was all in a tizzy. This was dangerous. We only had a couple things left to do for the fence to be finished. Sanding and painting–considering the snow would be flying again by monday, we didn't have much time. Then we would be strangers again.

My therapist, Sandra, told me I needed to find a way to be happy alone. But that had been months ago. *Am I happy?*

Would that include the dog?

No, Sandra was certainly not referring to a pet when she told me to be happy alone. The dog would help me get outside, more exercise. And I wanted to share my space and time with someone else. Even if that someone else was a fur ball that would potentially chew and drool all over everything.

When I awoke the next morning just rolling over in bed was an insurmountable task. Every bone, muscle, and ligament was telling me I should be on bed rest for at least the next week. Frowning, I checked my phone. I wasn't even sure what had caused me to wake.

It was just past eight, Lincoln said he'd be here at nine. Banging on the front door caused me to jackknife in bed and was followed by a few choice words. Lincoln could consider our tentative truce null and void if this was how he was going to knock on my door. Neither had killed the other the day before and I figured that counted for something.

Throwing my robe over my aching body I hobbled my way to the front door, swung it open ready to lay into the man for ruining my sleep. Except, the man in front of me had far too many gray hairs and one extremely disapproving scowl. Despite the pain, my spine stiffened on instinct causing me to wince. As I straightened to my full height I spotted the man I'd expected to see beyond the glowering one on my small porch.

Lincoln's brows pulled together in a silent question, or what I was going to assume was his way of asking if I was alright. *That would be a no.*

The frown slackened for a moment before falling back into its place on my father's face. "You all right?" he asked in his gravelly voice. Before he made his money he'd been a smoker and it showed through in the way his voice was more rumbled than it should be.

"I'm fine. To what do I owe this early morning visit?"

He folded his arms across his chest making me feel like the small disappointing child I'd always been. "After that conversation we had yesterday I knew I needed to drive myself to this hell hole and see what kind of trouble you were getting yourself into this time."

I felt as if I'd just been kicked in the stomach as all the air left my lungs. Balling my hands into fists, I glared into my father's deep blue gaze despite the ache in each of my fingers. "I was never the one to get in trouble as a child," I spat.

He harrumphed. "You were always supposed to come work for me."

"No, that's what you wanted." I paused to think if my next words were really necessary. "Besides it was Kendall you always wanted to come work for you, not me." The last two words were nearly a whisper. The old pain flaring again. There was only one daughter that was ever good enough in my father's eyes, despite the way I'd always done anything my parents asked.

Unbelievably my father's disapproval shone brighter. "Don't ever speak of your sister that way," he barked and then turned his back on me, much like he'd done most of my life.

Surprise, surprise.

The want to please my father and my new found confidence warred. Confidence won, or craziness depending on who was asked, I stomped down the steps behind him.

Lincoln's eyes grew wide, he'd continued to prep the fence for paint during mine and my father's verbal sparring match.

"Why was she your favorite?" I demanded as my legs burned, protesting against my near running pace.

My father halted as he reached for the handle of his black Mercedes. "What?"

"Why was she your favorite?" I asked again, folding my arms across my chest standing at the hood of my father's car. My chest was heaving with the deep breaths I tried to maintain.

"I did not have a *favorite*." His hand gripped the door handle causing his knuckles to pale.

"Is that so? Then why was it that you never seemed to be able to stand being in a room with me? I was never the daughter you wanted to spend your time with."

"I will not engage in a childish shouting match with you Kennedy."

With that he dropped into his car, started it and backed out of my driveway. Not once over the years had he asked me how I was doing, or how I felt. Instead he showed no interest in me, my happiness, or feelings. Today was just another day of animosity between us. But he'd shown up, that counted for something right?

My father rolled down his window before pulling away. "Get whatever this is out of your system. Then get back to work before the end of the month."

Only when the car had turned the corner did I release my fists, the proof of my frustration lay in my indented palms. Letting out a frustrated groan I spun on my heels to find Lincoln at the edge of the gate watching me like a hawk.

Flexing my hands I headed for the front door. "I'm going to make coffee, want some?"

His mouth opened and closed a few times before he spoke. "Sure."

With that I stepped inside, now embarrassed by the way I'd acted. Allowing my weight to fall against the door, I hit my head off the wood surface a few times. Looking down, another wave of embarrassment washed over me. I was in sleep shorts, a tank, and my mid-thigh length robe. Wonderful.

"Well the day can't get much worse," I muttered before pushing myself off the door and stomped to the kitchen.

The days when Kendall and I would run through parks together or study together were becoming faded memories. It was as if I were looking through a window at the memories, the sounds were muffled and the more I tried to focus on what I saw the heavier the rain would pelt the glass until all I saw were blurred outlines. Only the last good memory I had with my sister remained clear after all the passing years, but it also contained one of the worst memories of my life. We'd been at an ice cream window ordering our favorite sugary desserts. Mother had always had a soft spot for ice cream. I had just reached the height that I could see over the counter and was able to place my own order. Which was a monumental day in and of itself. But the other special part of the day was our mother telling us to order anything we wanted. And with how our parents usually struggled with money we'd never been told that before.

So, when we got to the counter we plotted together to make sure we could get the most of the day. Each would order one of the sundaes we always wanted and then we would share. That way, if it never happened again, at least we would be able to try two sundaes. We chatted excitedly about our classes at school and how excited we were about the rainbow sprinkles atop the whipped cream.

The sun was shining and we selected a picnic table next to a large tree that provided us plenty of shade. We shared our sundaes, as promised, while Mother watched. I was convinced our mother's eyes would rival any emerald in the world. I'd even thought that day how beautiful they were. They seemed brighter, but I hadn't realized the glaze in Mother's eyes were tears. Whether joy at the moment we shared or for the news she would impart on us later in the day I wasn't sure. I would never know.

I groaned as I was brought back to the moment by a searing pain in my hand. Running to the sink I held my hand in the freezing water pouring from the faucet. The skin was already reddening, how I'd poured the scalding coffee all over my hand rather than in the mug would be a mystery for a while but I shook off the pain and annoyance with myself.

This day can't get much worse than this...

Twenty minutes was how long I was always told to keep a burn under cold water, but I figured five was close enough. I doubted I should be doing anything today with how the day began and that is exactly what the old Kennedy would do.

I couldn't allow myself to wallow in my sadness, no, not the new Kennedy. I was going to face everything head on. Shying away from challenges was no longer an option. Or from my father. Confidence was going to be my new armor and I would wear it well. Putting distance between myself and my father was what I needed. Until he'd called the day before I'd been feeling vastly better about my life.

The balancing act I had to engage to get the door open meant I was nearly qualified to be in some sort of circus act. Perhaps I would try some little trick atop a horse next.

I stifled a laugh about my inner dialog, not wanting Lincoln to think I was any crazier than he probably already thought. If witnessing me crying after the unkind words my father sent my way in the parking lot of the hardware store wasn't enough, today he got to see the extent of our wonderful relationship. What a lucky man he was.

"Lincoln?" I called as I kicked the door shut behind me and descended the steps. It felt as if the hot coffee had a direct connection to the burn on my hand. The longer I held the beverage the more concerned I became that I would soon drop the mug on the concrete walkway.

"Here," he called, but I still couldn't see him.

The crunching of gravel in the driveway told me where to go. Rounding the garage I found him, his back to me, between our vehicles. Deciding his tailgate was as good a place as any, I dropped his mug down with a resounding thud. The burning sensation in my hand persisted. Dammit. I really needed to figure out how to be less clumsy. The thought had me rubbing the spot on my head where I hit it the day before. Still a little swollen.

Stepping around the corner of the truck I froze, at the sound of liquid hitting the stones. "Are you pissing in my driveway?" my voice came out at a near deafening pitch, equal parts loud and almost high enough only dogs would hear.

Lincoln's only response was a chuckle. "I am house broken but unlike a dog I do usually go to the bathroom in the house. Plus, if I had my dick out do you think I'd call to you?"

I blinked a few times, he had a point. "Then what are you doing?" I asked as a flush heated my cheeks. Great something else that was burning.

Lincoln turned around to face me lifting a gigantic metal water bottle. "I was looking for another pad for my sander, the package slid under the seat and I found my missing water bottle. I was dumping it when you came out."

I nodded, pursing my lips together. "Your coffees there," I said pointing.

Chapter Eight

Lincoln

ASIDE FROM KENNEDY AND her father getting into a rather heated argument the day had gone well. I'd banished Kennedy to safety monitor with a requirement of her holding ice on her burn after I saw it. As expected she didn't have a first aid kit or burn ointment. Taking a detour to my house during lunch I'd grabbed what I needed to clean up her hand and then finished our fence project.

She was all set up to get her dog.

Rolling my shoulders, I knew I needed to get home to make sure everything was set up so I could start boiling sap in the morning. The weekend had been a seasonal fluke. Snow would be coming back overnight. I'd been surprised by how much the ground had thawed and how easily we'd been able to dig the holes for the posts.

This new friendship was a bit awkward for me. I usually stuck to my own devices trying to make small talk with a virtual stranger while I kept as many of my dickish comments to myself, was difficult to say the least—almost painful. But after witnessing the weirdness between Kennedy and her father I didn't want to make it worse for her. So against all the cells in my body telling me to be a dick to prevent her from counting and relying on me, I tried to be nice and filter that wrecking ball of words that usually flew out of my mouth.

The last of my tools were in the back of my truck and Kennedy was standing behind me at the edge of her garage.

"Can I ask you something?" she asked at a near whisper as her cheeks flushed.

Fuck. When a woman acted like that I was usually more than happy to run the other way.

"I suppose." I knew the reluctance showed through in my voice. Solitude, that was what I liked, not heart-to-hearts with virtual strangers.

"What do you do?"

I relaxed, pressing more of my weight onto the tailgate of my truck. "I own a business and make various different goods throughout the year at my place," I said, hitching my thumb over my shoulder to indicate the road that led up to my house. "Going to start sugaring soon." I looked up at the cool blue sky. Not a cloud in sight, damn I needed the temp to drop.

And a good excuse to get away from this woman.

"As in making real maple syrup." Her eyes sparkled in the early evening sun. I should have kept my damn mouth shut.

"Yup." I pushed away from the truck, heading around the front to get in. On my way passed I didn't miss the way her face fell, the excitement that was there only a moment ago dissolved. Awesome. "I'm going to head home."

All she did was nod. She grimaced as she pulled off her work gloves. They must be sore and covered in blisters between the manual labor she wasn't used to and the coffee burns. *Who the hell needs their coffee that hot?*

She swiped the toe of one of her sneakers through the gravel in the drive.

"I need to install a doggy door too." She kept her gaze down on the ground as she spoke. After everything I'd done for her she didn't have the decency to look at me when she hinted at wanting more help?

Fuck this. "Is there a question in there somewhere?" My jaw was tense with annoyance.

She nodded, not looking up from her shoes. "Will you help me? I ordered one, I just don't know how to put the door in and stuff."

"Do you need me to shovel the dog's shit too or will you be able to handle that little detail?" Crap, and there's the wrecking ball, no longer accepting its constraints. Crumbling whatever we may have made as headway into a tentative friendship.

The silence stretched between us, I had expected her to send a zinging comeback right at me. One never came. Just when I thought I couldn't feel worse, she looked like I'd just told her the dog she was dreaming about was never going to come to be.

"Kennedy,"

"Don't, I don't know why you hate me so much but, you're free to go. I am trying to be a good neighbor, to get to know one another, but obviously that is not what you want. So after you're sure you have everything, please leave."

A feeling I hadn't had to experience in years of solitude took over my chest. An ache that threatened to bust my chest open settled in deep. "I want to help," I said before having time to think about what I was admitting.

Her glossy green eyes finally snapped up from her shoes. "You're giving me whiplash. You could at least act like it then. Instead of treating me like some kind of trash you found on the side of the road that you cannot wait to get away from. I may be a city girl but I am far from stupid, no matter what you or my..." She stopped herself as her chest heaved.

I ran my hands through my hair, "Look, I told you I'm not good with people. My first instinct is to push people away. I was trying to do better, get to know you."

"You haven't tried to get to know me, you've been an ass. I try to make conversation and I get minimal answers... I appreciate all your help. I really do, but if I have the choice between doing it alone and having a grumpy-flannel-wearing-dick," she said, waving her hand in my direction. "I'll do it myself."

Her cherry face and sad excuse for name calling made me chuckle, which was the wrong thing to do.

Kennedy spun around on the spot and stomped back into the house. I tried to banish the smirk from my face but I was failing when she reemerged from the house with something wrapped in plastic wrap. The plastic wrap log was slammed into my chest and I could smell the garlic and herb roasted turkey we'd eaten the day before.

"Have a great life."

I barely caught the sandwich before it dropped to the ground. "Kennedy, wait. I wasn't laughing at making you mad. I was laughing because of your terrible insults."

Well, that wasn't the right thing to say either, because she stomped into the house and slammed the door. But not before she tripped over the last step before making her way into the house. I had to force myself to suppress another laugh, this one was more warranted than the last but I knew she wouldn't take kindly to me openly laughing at her lack of coordination.

Taking my now smashed and potentially poisoned sandwich to my truck I headed home. I couldn't stop thinking about the way her face flushed whenever she got angry. It was both adorable and amusing.

Trudging up the pebbled path to my front door I let my ailing dog out the door. He no longer was able to follow me through the woods to check on all the taps and hoses strung between the trees. The thought saddened me as I ate in the chilly sugar house. Sap was running today, thankfully, the early thaw was a bit concerning.

"Do you want a doggy friend?" I asked, looking down at the only companion I'd counted on over the last several years.

Jax harrumphed and plopped down onto the floor with a long slow groan. I worried it was due to pain. Arthritis had started setting in and ever since Jax hadn't been the same. Saying goodbye to him was an inevitability in the far too near future.

Scratching the old mutt behind the ears, I sighed and then began cleaning up the sugar house. The holding tank was nearly full and I would need to start boiling soon. I couldn't wait to be surrounded by the heat and scent of sap boiling.

Kennedy's words kept running through his mind. I *am* trying to get to know her. Wasn't that obvious?

"What do you think Jax, do I go back and apologize, again?" As I cleaned the pan I knew I had to. There was more going on with her and, like myself, she could use someone else to lean on.

"Fuck me," I muttered as the realization sank in. I wanted to get to know her, wanted her to like me. It tasted bitter. The rest of the time I cleaned I consulted Jax about what I should do, with nothing more than a few groans and whines he did not add much to the conversation. As the sun set, it took the warmth from the air we trudged back inside.

I'd talk with Kennedy tomorrow. I'd show up in the morning. Did I need to bring anything to apologize for being an ass? Running a hand over my face I groaned. The evening was filled with far more stress over what I was going to say and if I should bring a peace offering that I didn't sleep. Or at least it felt like I hadn't.

Pulling in her driveway the next morning I held tight to the caramel macchiato the barista at the local cafe told me was Kennedy's regular. It burned my hand as I gripped it with all the anxiety in me as I reached for the doorbell.

Chapter Nine

Kennedy

My blood boiled through my veins as I prepared myself for the argument I'd had far too many times with my father. Since fifteen he had tried to turn me into what Kendall should have been, or what she would have been. Who knew now?

"You think you want to be with a man who won't be able to give you everything? That man didn't even look like he could afford the rattle trap of a truck he was driving."

My jaw clenched as I squeezed the phone tighter. "That man is my neighbor, nothing more nothing less. Even if I wanted him to be more to me, you get no opinion on that. He was here to help build a damn fence and.."

"Don't you speak to me that way. When this half baked idea of yours goes belly up you're going to need me, the job you left, and Brentley."

"Alright Brentley Gouldin cares about no one but himself and his image, he is the *last* person I would want to date. Second, I left that job because I *hated* it, being a paralegal was not for me, I never should have let you force me into that job and lastly," I paused as I heard someone on the front porch so I made my way around, knowing the possibility of my father standing there while on the phone was slim, but still terrifying. "I don't need you. I have the money I saved after mother's death. I mean, after all, I got not only my own but Kendall's inheritance too. So no, I don't need you, your money, or your damn job." Ripping the door open I was startled to find Lincoln standing on the threshold, wide eyed holding a paper coffee cup up to me.

My cheeks flushed as I imagined how my voice echoed through the, still mostly empty, house. The only person I was expecting this morning was Lydia from the dog shelter. She was supposed to be coming to do an inspection to ensure the property was safe and well secure for Tito.

Another argument with my father that Lincoln could have overheard. Fan-fucking-tastic. If it were possible for my throat to shrivel up to a raisin and drop into the pit of my stomach it would already be making its way through my intestines.

It wasn't until my father began to speak again that I remembered I was still on the phone. I continued to stare into Lincoln's ice blue eyes.

"You will see Kennedy; your mother and I only ever wanted what was best for you. Now you're throwing that all away. Kendall's and your mother's lives, wasted."

It felt as if he just punched me in the gut. That raisin that was settling into my middle shot back up into my throat to choke me. "Don't ever say that," I whispered, Kendall's smiling face jumped into my mind's eye. "Kendall would have played your games, and I tried," I forced my gaze to drop from Lincoln's as he shifted from one foot to the other. Part of me wanted to shut the door in his face, the other–lonely part–wanted to invite him in so he could bask in my misery with me. "But I am not her so please stop trying to force me to be." My voice cracked on the last word and I wished I'd been able to stay strong and angry.

Before I got more upset I hurried to continue, "Look Dad I have some things going on today, I gotta go."

"Bye, Kennedy..." I hung up before he could finish the thought. My gaze was focused on the disposable coffee cup that had a floral ring around the letters C.C.--Carla's Cafe–which had become my favorite coffee shop in town after I stumbled upon it while going for a walk one day.

I stared at the cup until Lincoln cleared his throat. "I ah, wanted to apologize for being an ass." The hesitation and fear in his deep voice had me raising an eyebrow.

I was in a sour mood already so I should force the words back down before they erupted. "And do you?"

His beard twitched in a small smirk. "Yes, I'm sorry Kennedy." He shifted again, "I ah, brought you a caramel macchiato as a sort of peace offering."

The man was clearly uncomfortable and I struggled with whether I should be making him work harder for my forgiveness or giving in to him right then and there. I never had been good at holding a grudge.

My lips twitched in a small smile as he extended the cup. "I was expecting you to get on one knee at least."

With a full on grin Lincoln dropped to one knee, "Kennedy I-don't-know-your-last-name, would you do me the honor of accepting my apology?"

I burst into laughter, which was far better than the tears that had been waiting in the wings, while taking the coffee. "Only because it's my favorite coffee." I said as I felt the pressure releasing from my chest.

"Do you want to come in?" I asked, pointing over my shoulder to indicate the living room.

Getting back to his feet he nodded and followed me in.

If I could have regretted a decision any faster I would be fast enough to beat a cheetah in a land race. Sitting on the back of my couch was the bra I'd discarded while reading the night before. And this was nothing that anyone in their right mind might consider sexy, so it was the last bra I would've wanted someone to see. This was the sports bra that supported me, literally, through my college track days. The yellowing on the originally white fabric only deepened my embarrassment. It was one of the most comfortable things I owned and when I got up the day before and knew more manual labor was on the menu I wanted something with support but no underwire.

Fuck. My. Life.

I nearly tripped as I awkwardly ran to the couch lunging to push the dirty scrap behind the back of the couch. I would fish it out later. This was not the time. I may be on shaky ground with Lincoln, but the last thing I wanted was for him to see my oldest, ugliest, and most used sports bra.

"Shit you okay?" Lincoln asked, stepping forward into the room, his brows were drawn close. "Did you just trip?"

I cleared my throat, amazed I hadn't lost a drop of coffee in my acrobatics. "No, well um, yeah kinda." He cocked his head to the side eyeing me suspiciously. Something fluttered to life in my middle and my cheeks were flaming. "Thank you for the coffee," I said, holding it up to block my face.

He chuckled and I couldn't deny I loved the sound. "Welcome." He rubbed a hand over the back of his neck. "I really do want to try and be friends or whatever."

"Or whatever? You may want to keep that part out the next time you say that to someone."

He nodded as he dropped down onto the couch, leaning back he rested his head right where my bra had been sitting. *Oh god, what if it smells sweaty.* Now that was all I was imagining, him finding my dirty sweat stained bra behind his head on the couch. If I wasn't already blushing I would be now.

"Seriously. Are you okay?" He shifted forward to rest his forearms on his knees holding his coffee in both hands like they were cold. "I didn't mean to interrupt anything when I got here." He cringed, as if sharing his thoughts was physically painful for him.

"You didn't interrupt, I was just about done anyway. I actually thought you were going to be Lydia."

"From the Shelter?"

"Yeah, you know her?"

He chucked and I could definitely get used to that sound. "Yeah, known her just about my entire life."

Something about that had a pang of jealousy raging through me. Tamping it down I reminded myself Lydia was married with children. The likelihood of her wanting the town grump was slim. *Wait, do I want the town grump?*

I took another sip of the heavenly coffee, examining the man in front of me. He was trying and that thought warmed me more than the scalding coffee I'd burned myself with the other day.

The doorbell rang and I all but leapt off the couch, smashing my shin into the coffee table in the process. I nearly cursed. Distance was something I needed. Lincoln was being kind to me and, after how rough my father had been with me, I could use kindness but I worried I was reading too much into it.

"Lydia," I said, smiling as I opened the door and pulled the slightly older woman into a hug. "Good morning, thank you for coming over on such short notice."

"Oh, no problem. I have Mondays off at the office. I will be heading to the shelter..." she trailed off as her eyes broke contact with mine and I again was assaulted with regret for letting Lincoln into the house.

It was barely nine in the morning and a man was sitting on my couch. Would people start to think we had something going on? "Ah, Lydia, Lincoln was kind enough to run to town this morning and get me coffee so I wouldn't miss you." It was a flat out lie and it made my stomach churn. It was true I didn't have to leave to get my own coffee but I made it sound like I'd asked Lincoln to do it. That might be even more grounds for her to think he'd stayed the night before.

I nearly groaned. The terrible liar award would soon be sitting on my living room mantle.

"Morning, Lydia. I wanted to make sure the fence we built was up to par for Kennedy to get her dog."

My shoulders sagged in relief. He was going along with it.

Lydia gave me a sly wink, "All right then, let's check it out." She spun on her heels heading back out the front door. The fence looked great, I was impressed with myself and Lincoln for everything we got completed in just two days.

I couldn't believe how we'd only, officially, met and actually talked to one another a few days ago, after I'd already been living here for two months.

I followed Lydia out and felt the heat of Lincoln's presence behind me. It sent a shiver down my spine. Part of me wanted to turn to see how close he was standing, while the other part wanted to keep my eyes ahead to make sure any potential thoughts Lydia might have about the two of us would dissipate. *That wink. I don't trust it.*

"This is fantastic guys!" Lydia exclaimed as she walked the border of the fence. "The only other thing you need is some space that is shaded for him."

"Oh, I am planning to get a doggy door. That way he can come and go as he needs."

"Yeah, we'll be putting that in soon."

My heart skipped at Lincoln's use of we.

Lydia nodded like this took a lot of thought. "He will still need something, just a small dog house. The shelter's regulations for adoptions are pretty strict," she said as if in apology. "But as soon as you do that we can get the paperwork signed."

I nodded bouncing on my toes. "Okay, I bet I can find one at that outdoorsy store."

Lincoln snorted behind me and I took the chance to look back and glare at him. Amusement continued to dance in his eyes as I did my best to look fierce. It was a wasted effort.

Lydia squeezed my shoulder, and I turned back to her. "You've done great." Her hand dropped and she turned. "Oh wait, did you want to go to those Zumba classes?"

I really wanted something to do with more of the women in the area, but I wasn't the most coordinated. I'd only done track in college because my father expected it and with it being his alma mater they let me join the team. I never competed, thank god, but I did enjoy running with them all.

Hurdles were my kryptonite. I nearly told Lydia so.

"Yeah, I think I will. Can you send me the address?"

"Sure hun. Lincoln, it wouldn't hurt you to get a social life too."

I caught him flip Lydia the bird.

Chapter Ten

Lincoln

"I FEEL LIKE I just need to get a job here, I'm here most days. Would I get an employee discount?" I asked Howard.

"Na, I'd start charging you even more."

I chuckled, shaking my head.

"I like seeing you happy again kid." Howard slapped a large hand on my shoulder.

I nodded. "Me too."

Squeezing my shoulder Howard asked, "That girl?"

Feigning ignorance sounded like a tempting idea but Howard would be able to smell a lie a mile away. Considering the man had known me since before I was out of diapers.

"She seems to be helping. I never know what she's going to do or say." I paused. "It's refreshing. For once, some girl doesn't already know my tragic past and didn't immediately try to talk to me about it."

Howard let his hand drop. "You should tell her before someone else does."

"I know," I said, rubbing the back of my neck.

"Why don't you come over and have dinner with us tonight."

Something clenched in my gut. I knew Mimi wasn't doing well. Howard wouldn't guilt me into attending but something told me I had to go. "What time?"

"Michelle likes to eat early, maybe five?"

"I'll be there," I said as the knot in my stomach crawled its way up to my throat, I hated it. The thought of losing someone else made me want to rage. To scream, worse yet, I wanted to cry thinking about losing Mimi.

Howard cleared his throat, "All right, what are you needin' today?"

"More lumber, making a dog house."

Howard's white caterpillars jumped farther up his forehead. "Not for your dog.."

Shifting from one foot to the other I shook my head. "For Kennedy."

"Hmmm."

"Don't start."

"Didn't say a damn thing," Howard said, raising his hands in surrender.

I shook my head, "Bullshit."

With another promise to be there for dinner, I headed to the lumber yard. I should be home making sure everything was ready to start boiling tonight but instead I was running secret errands for my new neighbor. *My annoyingly adorable neighbor.*

Connections and emotions were dangerous, and I knew I was quickly allowing myself to get sucked into the pit of quicksand.

I had to hope that I would either be able to pull myself out alone or have Kennedy help me up again.

Pulling back onto our dead end road, I ,for once, didn't have a strong visceral reaction to Kennedy's house. Insead of wanting to run away from it I wanted to stop, to see the firecracker who lived there. But she was at work.

Backing into the drive I would have just enough time to get the dog house built before I had to go to dinner and with any luck I could have it finished before I left and Kennedy got home.

After several hours of work, and running up to my house to find the leftover shingles from a roofing project a few years back, I was pleased with my finished product.

Kennedy would want to paint it and give it her own flare. Patting the top of the dog house I ran home to take my dog out for a walk and then got ready for dinner with Howard and Mimi.

That familiar stump took hold in my gut, wrapping its roots around my organs, braiding themselves in with my intestines. Stopping at the store on the way, I got some of Howard's favorite beers and Mimi's favorite wine. I didn't know if she would even drink it–if she could. I wasn't at all sure what the cancer was doing to her and how it was impacting all the things she'd loved.

I shook my head as I dropped from the truck cab. With the bottle of wine tucked under the arm holding the beers I checked my phone then started toward the front door. I had been checking my phone at regular intervals waiting for the moment Kennedy got home to find the new doghouse. Those roots tightened their grip as I thought of her not liking what I'd made.

This woman was turning me into a self-conscious middle schooler again. Worried what everyone was going to think of my braces.

Knocking once I let myself into the house to find Mimi standing at the stove while Howard hovered over her shoulder asking what he could do to help. The couple had been together more than fifty years. Longer than my parents had been alive. Another rough pinch–this one of jealousy.

It melted when Mimi looked up at me with those unbelievably soft eyes. "Lincoln dear, I have missed you." She wiped her hands off on the red and white gingham apron she always seemed to wear while cooking.

I found myself wondering if she had several or if she just washed this one everyday, because it never had a scrap of food on it. "Hey Mimi, I missed you too. Howard told me you were making your famous homemade pasta sauce. How could I resist?" I asked as I set the beer and wine on the table before I pulled her into a hug. Her small frame felt smaller than the last time I'd seen her. It was as if she was withering away right in front of my eyes.

"You're right on time. I am nearly done, dear." She patted my cheek and turned back to the stove, she looked like she was having a good day today. "Now, go set the table," she said as she retrieved the wooden spoon from the rest on the back of the stove.

"Yes, Mimi," I said, moving the beer and wine to the counter and began pulling plates and silverware from drawers. The house was small, but it was just the two of them so the small space was fine. The window over the sink faced the front yard where Mimi's flower beds were buried under the layer of snow they'd gotten the night before. Small dead leftovers from last year's blossoms stuck up through the snow. And I didn't know why, but it was reminiscent of a head stone sticking out of the ground. Rolling my shoulders I went about my task, refusing to look out that window again. There was an ominous feeling about it.

When we were all seated, our chatter came easy as it always had.

Mimi in her usual tactless manner jumped into her questioning. "So, tell me about this girl I've heard you've been spending all your time with?" There was almost a jealous tone to her question.

I nearly choked on my garlic bread and Howard was smiling into the beer he was sipping on. The wine remained unopened. "I was spending time with her because your *husband*," I said, shooting a pointed look at Howard, "volunteered me to help build her a damn dog fence."

Howard's grin widened.

I tipped my head from side to side trying to think of the best way to describe it. "Good for the most part," I said around another bite of the bread. The ratio of butter to garlic and the crispiness was perfect. "It was weird, her father stopped in the other day." I paused furrowing my brow, wondering if this was too much to share. It wasn't my story to tell and I hated people talking about me behind my back. So, I kept it short. "Something just seemed off between them."

"You be nice to that girl," she said, pointing a gnarled finger at me, almost accusingly.

"I didn't do anything," I insisted like a child being scolded.

"Make sure it stays that way."

Howard chucked, "Michelle met her the other day while shopping. She likes her."

"She was sweet, carried my groceries right out to my car, even loaded them."

I couldn't suppress a smile–that sounded like Kennedy.

"Granted she dropped the bag that had the eggs in it, sending them rolling and smashing all over the parking lot."

Howard broke into a full belly laugh, "You know Mrs. Fred-don, who always yelled at you if you cut across her lawn on your way to the post office for me?"

I nodded.

"She was just getting out of her car at the store," Howard's voice was coming in quick spurts as he tried to keep back his laughter.

Mimi hit her husband's arm with her napkin, in a way of jest and admonishment. "You stop it."

"What the heck happened?" I asked eager to find out what happened to the rude old hag.

Mimi huffed while trying to suppress her own laugh. "Fine," she said then cleared her throat and tried to wipe the smile from her face as she swiped her napkin over her mouth. "Well, Mrs. Freddon, was making her way around her car while your Kennedy was loading my bags into my trunk. I am not sure how she did it, but somehow she hit her elbow off the edge of the cart at the same moment Mrs. Freddon was tucking her reusable bags under the cart she'd retrieved from the spot next to her. The bag toppled, dumping first the loaves of bread over her head, but then the eggs came."

Howard was nearly howling with laughter as Mimi lost composure with each word she spoke.

"I was planning to make cookies for the kids that do the cleanup at the church, on Sundays. So I had a dozen and a half eggs in that bag, no less than five broke over Mrs. Freddon's head.

"By the time the rest had fallen to the ground and either miraculously rolled away Mrs. Freddon was standing at her full height face the closest to tomato red I've ever seen."

I was imagining the entire scene playing out, the look of shock that was likely on Kennedy's face as she realized what she'd done. And in turn the tantrum I was sure Mrs. Freddon had.

I was laughing so hard I had to swipe a tear from the corner of my eye. "I wish I had been there."

"You and me both," Howard said as he pulled his handkerchief out of the front pocket of his flannel.

"Anyway, she probably scared the life out of that poor girl of yours."

Something in me loved the way Mimi kept referring to her as mine. "When was this?" I leaned back on two legs of the chair I'd been told hundreds of times not to do.

Mimi tapped her fingers on the table as she thought. "Last Friday I think."

That was the same night I'd found Kennedy stuck in the mud in the middle of our road. If there were a contest to see who could get themselves into the most ridiculous situation she would take the cake.

Just as the thought crossed my mind, Mimi brought a double chocolate cake to the table. It looked amazing, my mouth began to water just thinking about taking a slice. Mimi served the cake as Howard and I removed the dinner dishes and took care of leftovers.

As we settled back into our chairs the laughter from the moments before had completely evaporated and that ominous feeling was back. Tangling in my middle again. My hosts' demeanours changed as I picked up my fork. I was determined to take at least one bite before I was accosted with whatever they were about to drop.

The cake was just as decadent as it looked.

Mimi fidgeted with her fork, "I have something I need to tell you dear." Her somber tone was enough to freeze my fork before it made it all the way back to my plate.

As she spoke some of my worst fears, Kennedy's name lit up on the screen of my cell phone. As if she could sense that I was getting some of the most awful news of my life.

Mimi had been given six more months to live.

Chapter Eleven

Kennedy

THE FACT THAT I came home the day before to see a dog house in the fenced in yard had my heart melting like the snow from the eves. I would be able to adopt, I was so close.

Going to work the last few days this week was going to be difficult knowing what the weekend would bring. I would finally have him. Everything seemed to be working out for me for once—nearly everything anyway.

I'd texted Lincoln what I thought was a heartfelt thank you but had heard nothing. Now I was overthinking what I'd texted him as I read it again wondering if the tone was off. But it was a damn thank you, obviously the tone would be gracious.

Making friends had never been easy for me, people either took advantage of my kindness or thought I was trying to get something from them. It was so strange. People never seemed to just want to be my friend. It was these moments I wished for Kendall. Losing my other half had been so difficult and I wished I could just talk with her one more time; get her opinion on Lincoln, he was definitely different. He went out of his way to help me, he'd been an abrasive ass at first but he was warming up to me. That meant something.

Or so I thought.

How pushy would it be to text him again?

I groaned as I shifted my car into drive and took off for work. I could worry about Lincoln later, but he would be in the back of my mind all day.

Arriving at the chiropractor's office I was surprised to find that Mel's car was not in the parking lot and neither was Dr. Anderson's too sporty car for the dirt roads of Vermont. I paced the parking lot for a few minutes, I didn't have a key to the building because I had never needed one. One or both of them was already there before I arrived each morning.

As I was climbing back into my car, my phone began to ring.

Mel's name shone bright on the screen.

"Hello?"

"Kennedy, hi, I have been at the hospital all night with Dr. Anderson," Mel blurted in a hurried breathless manner.

I gasped, "Oh my, is he okay?"

"Yes and no."

My head fell against the headrest. "What does that mean?"

"He was in a car accident last night. Someone ran a red light and T-boned the doctor. Broke his left arm and fractured his left femur."

"Oh no," I was at a loss for words.

"Right, so the Doctor will be out of work for several weeks. They aren't entirely sure how long he will need the casts," she hiccupped and I wondered if she was crying. "They say older bones take longer to heal."

I found myself nodding, not entirely sure what I was going to do. A new job was now in order. The chiropractor's office was never meant to be my end game, but I wasn't anticipating needing to find a new job within a few months of being here.

"I am heading to the office now to call all patients and let them know there will be an extended delay in getting them in," Mel said hesitating. "You should try to find something in the meantime."

"I will." Disconnecting the phone I was in shock. I'd never been without a job. I had this one lined up before I left working for my father. And now ,for the first time, I knew what it felt like to not know how I was going to pay my bills. Asking my father for help was out of the question.

None of the seasonal jobs would be operating again until summer. Groaning, I knew one thing was for certain–I was not going to call my father.

Pulling up one of the job sites I tried to filter the junk from the real jobs.

As I was pulling up the requirements for a personal assistant job nearly thirty minutes away someone tapped on my window. I screamed and almost threw my phone into the windshield. Mel's face looked apologetic through the glass. Probably for more than just the near heart attack.

I rolled the window down to talk to the older woman.

"Sorry, hun didn't mean to startle you." She had never called me hun before. She'd never even been this nice to me.

"It's okay."

"I was going to call you after I got here," Mel said and I remembered she was very strict about her no phone use while driving. I didn't quite understand that one. Sure she made sure to be hands free, but if her phone was connected to her car's speakers she'd answer calls while she was driving.

"Oh?"

"I was talking with my friend Norma who works as a cashier at Pete's Grocer down on main street. They had a cashier walk out and quit Saturday. They will be looking for someone."

I nodded, I'd never run a cash register in a store like that. Sure I ran people's cards at the chiropractors office but I didn't have to weigh anything to determine the price and I definitely wasn't outgoing. I began to fidget with the edge of my scrubs.

"I'll look into it, thanks Mel."

"Sorry, I know this might put a wrench in your plan for that dog."

Something sank lower in my middle. I hadn't even thought what this would do to my chances of adopting Tito. Or my health insurance.

"Good luck," Mel said and then turned on her heel.

Releasing a long slow breath I braced myself for the inevitable. It was time for a change, whether I wanted it or not. I'd only ever held three jobs in my life. Working at the chiropractors office, bookkeeping for a small family owned store, and my father's law firm. The last was a place I never wanted to return to, so I had to make the best possible choices for myself at the moment. Being a cashier couldn't be that bad. I just needed to learn how to be more outgoing. The thought of having to work with and around people in such a setting was already making my palms sweat. Wiping my hands on my baby pink scrubs I decided it would be best to go home, change and then go to the store to ask about the position.

I told myself it was so I could look professional, but really it was more about mental preparation. So long as I didn't chicken out before getting back in my car.

Pulling outfits out of my closet, I couldn't decide what said 'I need this job' more than any of the rest. All my pencil skirts and blazers would be way too much for such a position. The last time I'd been in the store I was pretty sure the woman who scanned me through the checkout was wearing sweatpants. Which was both a relief and a little anxiety inducing.

Looking pretentious was not on my list of things to do. With a groan I pulled on a soft scoop neck sweater and a pair of dark wash jeans. An outfit I'd never worn while attempting to get a job, my father would likely drop dead.

I twisted my dark, auburn hair into a quick braid and headed back out to the car. The time really did help me wrap my mind around the idea of having to be around people more. It was one thing to check people in at the chiropractor's office or to be in a one-on-one meeting where I asked them questions. But being in a wide open space where any mistake could be seen by so many made my skin crawl.

Just imagining how uncomfortable it would be to tell someone their card was declined had me feeling bad for the imaginary customer. Then again, if I didn't get this job that could be me. The money I'd used to buy the house was spoken for and I had too much in student loans to take too much time off from work. My nest egg would be gone far too soon.

Exhaling, I headed back out to my car. One glance at the fenced in yard and the dog house told me I was doing the right thing. Going outside my comfort zone was necessary sometimes.

The drive to the store was filled with too many invasive thoughts to ever be comfortable. My stomach was now twisted into a pretzel and I didn't think I would ever be able to come into the store to shop if I couldn't get the job.

The automatic glass doors revealed the manager leaning against the end of the first cashier's bagging area. He was in his mid fifties at least, his temples were feathered with gray hair while the rest was nearly black. The high and tight haircut hid most of the grays.

He turned as I stepped in, smiling at me, "Good morning."

Instantly I felt as if I no longer had a voice. Clearing my throat I tried again and extended my hand. "Hi, my name is Kennedy and I was told you may be looking for a new cashier."

The man took my hand in his, and it was rougher than I was expecting. After all, he worked in an office. "Yes, we lost a cashier over the weekend. It is not supposed to be in the paper until Saturday, but small towns." He shrugged as if to say he wasn't surprised I was there to ask about the job.

"Would you be able to talk about the position?"

"Absolutely, do you have a resume?"

I nodded, letting my purse fall from my shoulder, withdrawing an envelope with the new resume I'd printed just before leaving. Embarrassment filled my cheeks to see the way my hand trembled as I handed it to him.

"Why don't you come to the office with me, tell me a little about yourself, and then maybe I can save a little money by not having to post that help wanted ad?" He chuckled as I followed him around the front of all the registers to a door in the corner of the building, I'd never noticed before.

Taking one last look over my shoulder, the older woman at the register we'd just left gave an encouraging smile. The small gesture from a stranger had some of the tension I was experiencing ebb slightly.

"Okay, Kennedy, I don't know if I introduced myself before; I am Matthew. But you can call me Matt," he said as he sat down behind his desk and gestured for me to take the seat across from him. "Now, please let me know what you believe makes you good for this position."

Once again it was as if my ability to speak vanished. Taking a calming breath I explained how I'd once been a bookkeeper so I was good with math and had a good attention to detail. What helped was that most of my jobs had some sort of customer facing time.

"I won't lie, I am not entirely comfortable with the thought of talking with customers, but I am a quick learner."

Matt nodded as he flipped through my resume again. "You have a law degree. Why do you want to work in a small grocery store?"

"I found the family business wasn't well suited for me."

He looked doubtful.

"And I love the area, this town."

Chapter Twelve

Lincoln

THE LAST TWO DAYS I'd been existing in a fog. The revelation that Mimi had only been given another six months to live weighed heavily. With everything I'd lost I didn't want to think about losing anyone else. My parents. My grandparents. Now Mimi.

They didn't want to lie to me but I was having a difficult time stomaching the reality of the situation. And the worst part was Kennedy had reached out to me twice. The moment I saw her message thanking me for the dog house, Howard and Mimi were telling me her prognosis.

"Fuck, Jax." I ran a hand over my hair as I strapped the snow shoes on. "I'll check on her when I get back," I promised the dog who was trying to sit nearly on top of the wood stove in the sugar shack. I would walk my lines, make sure they were all in good order, and then go see if she was home from work. Maybe then I would tell her what's been on my mind.

Howard was right the other day, I needed to tell her before someone else did. Especially if I thought we might be able to be friends. That's where I would draw the line. I had too much to lose to let it be anything more. The more involved we became the worse it would be when she eventually left. We're neighbors, I would have to have some interactions with her.

There were a few taps I had to replace but the lines were in good condition.

By the time the sugar house came back into view I was panting and my legs were nearly entirely made of jello. A scream had me rushing down to the building. The door was open and I was willing to bet the scream had come from Kennedy.

It was certainly that of a woman and she was the only person I could readily think of that had zero regard for my personal space. Coming down the knoll I was trying to move too quickly. I stepped on the back of one snowshoe with the other, causing me to lose balance and in turn had me somersaulting down the remainder of the hill.

I came to an abrupt halt when I rolled into the trunk of an old tree. I groaned as I sat up. There was snow in more crevasses than I wanted to think about and my back was throbbing like a bitch. I pinched my eyes shut trying to ignore the pain that was radiating down my spine. I needed to get up. The snow was already seeping through my clothes.

Opening my eyes I narrowed them on Kennedy's small form shaking. Maybe she was cold.

"Are you all right?" her voice was faltering.

"I'll be fine." I didn't think I'd ever embarrassed myself quite so thoroughly in front of a woman. "Are you cold?" I asked sitting up to unstrap the shoes and stretch out my back. I was pretty confident nothing was broken, but I would be sore for the next few days.

"Un-uh." she said, shaking her head.

"Then why are you shivering?" Just as the question left my lips and I stood, I realized she was laughing. "Are you fucking laughing at me? I could have fallen to my death and you're laughing?" I did my best to sound annoyed.

She scoffed, "There was no way you were going to die tumbling down that hill." She jutted one hip to the side and placed her hands on them as if she were about to scold me.

Walking down the last of the hill, I tried my best to hide the limp. If I'd taken that roll down the hill a few years ago I was convinced there would have been no repercussions.

Still barely holding it together Kennedy asked, "Are you sure you're all right?"

"Positive," I grumbled. "Why the hell were you screaming anyway?"

Her laughter danced through the air between us as her cheeks flushed scarlet.. "Oh, I didn't know you had a dog, so when I opened the door he startled me. How come you never mentioned him?"

I shrugged. It was a strange thing to not bring up considering all the time we'd spent getting her place ready for her dog. Her smile faltered for a moment, she was quick to bring it back. That moment of hurt. It made me feel like a heel. I hadn't done anything wrong but I still couldn't suppress that feeling of not being a good friend. Already. Great.

"I think we need to get you warmed up and into some dry clothes."

I nodded, "C'mon Jax." I leaned the snowshoes up against the edge of the building. "Do you, ah," I rubbed the back of my neck at a loss. "Want to come in?"

In a moment the fake smile turned genuine and it heated me from the inside out. The realization told me this was dangerous. Her inside my house was not going to be a good idea. But it was too late now, right?

"Yeah, that would be nice," she said, nodding. She bent over scratching Jax behind the ear and his tail wagged in a testament to his own excitement.

I could do this, I just needed to keep my distance–emotionally and physically. If that were still even an option. The way my heart stuttered while watching her fawn over my ancient dog wasn't a good sign. Doomed. That's what I was when it came to this woman.

As I led the way from the sugar shack to my house I couldn't help but wonder if I'd known this was going to happen; if that was perhaps why I tried so hard in the beginning to keep distance between us.

The entire way up the hill and around the drive Kennedy seemed to be keeping a full fledged conversation going with Jax. The old dog was so happy to have someone else to spend time with. Before his hips started to have problems I took him to the store and nearly every other place with me.

But, old age and all.

"Lincoln?"

Shaking my head, I turned to look at the woman who was taking up far too much space in his brain–and quite possibly my heart. "Sorry, what did you say?"

"I asked you if you were sure you're all right. You're limping."

I furrowed my brow and looked down at myself as if it were going to give me a hint. I shrugged, "I think so, I don't feel like anything really hurts."

Kennedy didn't look like she was convinced but I took the last few steps into the house. It was an old farmhouse, where my grandparents had lived after they got married. There was something about the old place that made me feel just that little bit closer to them. The floors needed replacing and the cabinets could use it too; I just have a hard time removing what they had built. My grandfather built the house from the ground up, and replacing anything felt like I was removing a piece of them.

Heck, when I had to replace the damn putrid avocado green refrigerator I felt bad. The thing had been bought a couple decades before I'd been born and I knew my grandfather put a lot into it over the years to keep it working. But when the man who used to help my grandfather finally said there was no way to replace the parts, I had to accept defeat and have it hauled away. Only to wish I hadn't and had instead turned it into a cooler for all the parties I didn't host.

"This place is so cute." Kennedy traced a finger along the hand painted flowers on the front of the cabinets. One of the details my grandmother had added to the place. Painting was one of her favorite hobbies and my grandfather was always game for any of her ideas.

"Thanks, this used to be my grandparent's place." Now that I was warming up, the aches began to settle in. "I am going to get out of these wet clothes. I'll be back," I said, backing out of the room.

Kennedy smiled and nodded. She was standing in the kitchen in fuzzy socks. They looked like something you'd wear if you were trying to slide across a waxed floor. The image of Kenendy doing so was adorable and slightly terrifying. Mostly terrifying. Because I wanted to watch her, and be there to catch her when she inevitably went too fast.

The wet fabric of my jeans was beginning to bother my legs. Sitting on the edge of my bed I removed my pants to find I had a large bruise on one of my knees. It was tender. I should put some ice on it. Wearing shorts and a fresh tee shirt and flannel, I would not be part of any fashion shows anytime soon.

Hobbling into the bathroom, I plucked a washcloth from the shelf to create a makeshift ice pack.

"Damn, that's a good one." Kennedy looked over her shoulder from in front of the old gas stove.

"Probably from hitting that damn tree."

Kennedy giggled, "Must be you've been around me too much."

"Why, because I can't walk without hurting myself?" I quipped.

She smirked. "I see you're catching on. I can trip over nothing and everything all at the same time." She turned back to the stove as I filled a baggie with ice and propped myself up on the counter.

All in the span of a few seconds she stubbed her toe, nearly burned herself, and hit the top of her head off the hood over the stove.

"Are you sure it's safe for you to be in there? Near open flames? Plus, what are you making?"

"It's fine." She rubbed the spot on the top of her head. "I'm just not used to your kitchen yet."

Yet. I liked the sound of that a little too much.

"Anyway, get out of the kitchen; go sit down and ice that," she said pointing to the already too purple spot on my leg. "I saw the tea bags on the counter and figured something warm to drink would be good for you," her cheeks turned rosy. "To warm up."

"Why are you blushing.." I stopped myself before I blurted out a pet name I shouldn't be using. This was getting ridiculous.

"Nothing," she mumbled as she fumbled through the cupboards, likely searching for cups. The fact that she just came in and started making herself at home doesn't even annoy me.

"I had to find a new job–at the grocery store." She poured the hot water into the mugs she'd pulled down from the cabinet. Cursing when some of the water splattered onto her hand.

I'd heard about the doctor's accident, I'd forgotten she worked for him.

"The manager tried to gossip about you."

My breathing stopped immediately.

Chapter Thirteen

Kennedy

I PLACED ONE OF the mugs of tea on the coffee table in front of Lincoln as his spine went ram-rod straight. His reaction was enough to tell me I'd done the right thing.

"I told Matt I didn't want to gossip about you and that you were a friend. If there was something that had happened and you wanted me to know you'd tell me." Putting him on the spot like this was hard but I had to know if he trusted me. I was not a dishonest person and I didn't want to know something about him that he didn't want me to know.

"Did he give you any hints?" The anger on Lincoln's face was terribly unsettling.

"He started to say that you had an unconventional upbring-ing from a young age. When I didn't appear to know what he was talking about he said you were likely traumatized as a child. I stopped him there before he could go any farther."

Lincoln scoffed. "You could say that again."

I remained standing, not wanting to intrude if he wanted to drink his tea alone. If he said so, I would turn and leave. He shifted on the couch, balancing the bag of ice on his knee. He took his tea and sat back against the cushions. His eyes remained closed for a long moment and I took the chance to take a sip of my scalding tea.

When he opened his eyes again the pain there had tears welling in my own.

"Please don't feel like you have to tell me anything. I just want you to know I will wait until you're ready to tell me your story or I won't hear about it. I will not take the information from someone else." I was a firm believer in the fact that people deserve privacy.

Lincoln shot me a sad smile and patted the cushion next to him. "I was actually thinking today that I needed to tell you before someone else took the opportunity from me."

Settling down next to him I inhaled his woodsy scent, but it was mixed with something else. It was a little musty, maybe the smell of the sugar shack.

"It is true that I didn't grow up in the most conventional situation, although it had been the reality for many kids. I grew up here with my grandparents from the age thirteen on. Before that I lived with my parents. It was their anniversary and they were going out to dinner." He took a sip of his tea.

I had a terrible feeling I knew where this was headed.

"They were going to the same restaurant where they had their first date. It was one of the first times I was allowed to stay home alone, I was so fucking proud of myself. Anyway, they said they'd be home by ten and so I stayed up in my bedroom waiting for them to come home. When they came in they were loud.

Which was unusual because they, most of the time anyway, tried to be quiet if there was a chance I was sleeping. So I got out of bed to go say goodnight to them. When I got to the kitchen I heard my mother begging my father for something. I couldn't understand her but she sounded off. Scared." He closed his eyes, and took a deep breath.

My stomach became a knotted mess.

"I turned the corner and saw that my father had my mom pinned to the kitchen counter, at first I thought they were up to things I wouldn't want to see so I started to step back, but that was when I saw the gun at her temple and I froze. Part of me wanted to jump at him. To try and take the gun away from him.

"He was yelling at her about something to do with hitting on all the men they saw and she was crying, telling him she would never do that. He slapped her across the face and I stepped forward. That was when they noticed me. My mother looked horrified. She told me my dad drank too much, as blood was trickling down the side of her head. She told me I needed to go to bed but what I really wanted to do was call the police. My father told me not to go anywhere." Lincoln's voice cracked.

The sound had Kennedy's heart following suit.

Clearing his throat he continued, "My mom just kept yelling at me that I needed to run, to get out of there. But I was frozen with indecision. Did I try to overpower my father who was twice my size? Did I try to take the cordless house phone out of the docking station at the edge of the kitchen and hope he wouldn't see me? Or did I just go to bed and act like nothing more was happening. Before I could do anything my father got sick of her cries and hit her again. This time her body went limp and I lunged at him.

"I just tried to tackle him. The gun he had went off and grazed the upper part of my arm. I was so surprised I stumbled back. I put my hand to my arm, when I pulled it back to look at it, blood dripped to the floor and I screamed. That brought my mother back from being knocked out.

"She never asked what happened, she looked from my arm to my father then to the gun. She let out a scream that haunted my dreams for years and started swinging at him. I don't know how many times she hit him; it all happened so fast. One moment she was scratching at his face, the next there was another loud bang, and a moment later she was nothing but a crumpled pile on the floor."

A gasp escaped my lips. Without thinking, I extended a hand and took Lincoln's free one in mine.

"My father's face turned white and lost all expression. He kept whipping his head between me and my mother. Finally he looked at me and said he was sorry. Without warning he put the barrel of the gun in his mouth and one more shot rang out. The rest of the night is a blurry mess. I still, to this day, don't remember calling the police but they say I did.

"The day following that I moved into this house with my Mother's parents. I had only met them a handful of times because my father was such a controlling ass. He didn't like my mother visiting her own parents, and then he took her away from them. Permanently."

"And you," I whispered, squeezing his hand, his eyes met mine and it was as if I was looking into the soul of that same little boy.

He nodded. "So I lived here with them and then my," he had to clear his throat. The story clearly didn't come to him easily, I wondered how many people he'd shared this story with over the years. "Then my grandmother got ill. It happened so quickly. It was like one day she felt weak while we were at the grocery store and the next thing I knew she was hardly able to walk from her bed to the bathroom."

The pain of loss took over my heart. "I'm sorry, Lincoln." The words felt as if they were worth less than the dirt on the bottom of my shoes. "What about your grandfather?" I asked hesitantly, I was afraid of the answer.

A sad smile crossed his lips. "My grandparents were considered old when they had my mother, so thankfully he passed of old age. Really the only family member I have ever known to do so," he said scoffing as he finished.

The urge to apologize again for a past I never could have prevented was on the tip of my tongue. He squeezed my hand before the words left my lips as if he knew what I was about to say.

"I haven't talked about the entire story with anyone in a long time," He said, taking one last sip from his tea before placing it on the coffee table.

Emotion got lodged in my throat. I wanted to say I understood the need to keep the stories of how loved ones' lives ended to yourself. Not always wanting to share what happened. It changed the way people looked at you when you shared your trauma. Sometimes irreparably. Since words were failing me it was my turn to show my support with a gentle squeeze on his arm. We sat in companionable silence for a few minutes.

I would tell my story another time. I didn't want it to feel like it was a trade or that I was comparing traumas. If I had to venture a guess I would say he suffered more than I had.

Releasing his hand I took our mugs to the sink. "How's that leg?"

Lincoln winced as he pulled the makeshift ice pack off and leaned forward to glance at the bruise. "Looks like a damn eggplant already."

I couldn't suppress the laugh that burst at what people had been using eggplants to describe lately.

"Kennedy," he all but growled. "I am talking about my leg."

"I didn't say anything." My face flushed as I sat back down next to him.

"I know what that damn giggle was about. I know what people use the eggplant emoji for." The smirk and eyebrow raise he was giving me had something funny happening with my insides.

"I have no idea what you're talking about. What do people use the eggplant emoji for?" The question would go one of two ways, and the latter meant my already burning face was likely to turn a deeper shade of crimson than I assumed it already was. Joking around was more comfortable than the seriousness of the moments before.

Lincoln's smirk widened into a full fledged grin. "From the way your cheeks have continued to turn a deeper shade of red I am going to call bullshit on that one. Unless you'd like me to make you turn into a cherry by explaining it."

I shifted on the couch. "Nope. You don't have to."

Lincoln chuckled as if he'd won. Maybe this one, but there would be other opportunities. There must be something that would make him blush too. I just needed to figure out what that was.

Lincoln grimaced as he shifted on the couch. "Did you want to watch a movie?"

If being awkward were a superpower, I would be lighting up the sky like a beacon. For some reason if he had just turned something on it wouldn't have felt so monumental. But he asked, and now I was questioning if I'd overstayed my welcome. Ahh my overthinking was still fully intact. My impromptu visit had seemed like a good idea when I left the store.

Now?

Now, it felt like I was being put on the spot. My therapist specifically told me I needed to find a way to be happy alone, but that had been when I first left my ex. Would this count? He wasn't asking me to marry him after all. Just a movie.

Apparently he could sense my indecision and he placed a hand on my knee. Effectively stopping the bouncing I didn't even know was happening. "Absolutely no pressure Kennedy. You look like a caged animal right now. Why don't I just drive you back home? It's too dark to walk."

Chapter Fourteen

Lincoln

THE MORNING SOMEHOW FELT easier than usual, I had an unusual spring in my step; figuratively since one leg was the color of a damn cartoon dinosaur. Talking about my family and all the issues made me feel more than I had in a long time. The way Kennedy choked when I asked her to watch a movie was a little strange, but I was still happy with how the night had gone. I am turning into a pushover. If any other woman had shown up uninvited I would have chased her away. A shiver ran over my body as I thought of the last woman I'd dated.

With Mimi not doing well I was torn on if I wanted to bring new people into my circle.

Because, like everyone else, I would just lose them at some point. Rolling my shoulders, I tried to get back into the improved mood I woke up in. There was a lightness to me today that was energizing. Given my state, I took the morning to complete all the chores I'd been procrastinating on getting around to.

Walking anywhere today was going to be a bitch. I'd iced it well the night before but my knee was still swollen, purple, and at times had its own pulse that could rival the bpm of a jackhammer. The chilled air made the pain worse somehow. I thought it would dull it, instead it was amplified with an ache I couldn't shake. I was grateful that I had boiled the sap I'd collected earlier in the week. I might be able to manage another couple days before needing to boil again.

Taking Jax outside had been more of a pain than I thought it would.

I wanted to reach out to Kennedy and ask her about her morning. Would that be weird? I didn't even know how to conduct myself around a woman anymore. The last time I took someone on a date had been over six years ago.

Groaning, I fed Jax and sipped my coffee.

"You liked her didn't you, Jax?"

The old dog barely looked up from his bowl before diving back in. The one thing that hadn't changed over the years was the gusto with which Jax ate.

Pulling my phone out I decided eight in the morning was not too early to send a text.

Lincoln: *Are you still picking up your dog today?*

Once the message was sent I couldn't help but wonder if I should have said good morning first. Why had I jumped directly into a question? Making myself another cup of coffee I checked the screen.

Nothing.

I hadn't been this obsessed with getting a message back from someone since I was in high school. Shaking my head I decided a shower may be good for my sore muscles. Allowing the hot spray to run over my aching body, I had to be careful with my damaged knee.

Shutting the water off I jumped when my ears were assaulted by the doorbell ringing on repeat. Hastily, I stepped out of the shower. Missing the foam mat, my wet foot hit the cold tile and it nearly came out from under me. My only savior was the towel rack by the shower.

"The fuck, is someone dead?" I growled, then cringed at my word choice as I ripped the towel from the rack and wrapped it around my waist. Making my way to the door, I decided I was going to murder whoever was on the other side and thought ringing a doorbell on repeat for more than three minutes was acceptable.

Flinging the front door open I found myself looking down at the woman who was somehow a massive pain in my ass and the brightness to my days. Her eyes went wide as she looked over my body. When her eyes reached mine, her face flushed and then she narrowed her eyes at me.

"What the fuck are you doing?" I asked at a near shout. Too angry to enjoy the embarrassment she obviously felt over me answering the door nearly nude.

Kennedy balled her hands into fists placing them on her hips. "You don't remember." Now she seemed pissed, great.

"Remember what?" I growled, "Also, you do realize ringing a doorbell once is usually sufficient, right? I nearly did some tendon ripping acrobatics in the bathroom getting out of the

shower to come see what the hell kind of fire was happening."
The angry crease between her brows dissolved for a moment
before she narrowed her eyes again. "Damn, it's cold out. Get
in here and tell me what the hell I did. Or didn't do." I turned,
leaving the door open, and went to the bathroom to pull on
sweatpants and a t-shirt. All the while I tried to think of what I
was supposed to remember.

Emerging from the bathroom I found Kennedy standing by
the front door, arms crossed over her chest in her puffy black
vest and pale pink sweater.

Mimicking her stance I asked her what the hell I forgot.

"You told me last week you would help me get the doggy door
installed," she said, dropping her hands and balling them into
fists again. "Now, I am going to either have to skip it, or be late
for work."

"Fuck," I muttered letting my head fall back into the wall. "I
wish you had reminded me last night."

Her eyes glossed over and looked like she was about to cry. An
angry Kennedy I could handle, the crying version not so much.
When I was the reason for someone's tears I lost all sense of what
I should do.

"What if they don't let me have him because I don't have
that damn doggy door?" she asked, nearly hysterical as the tears
began to flow.

"They won't deny you if you don't have a fucking door installed, Kennedy. That sounds ridiculous."

Logic was obviously the wrong thing to point out to her at this point, because she just started crying harder.

Running a hand through my damp hair I let out a long slow breath. Stepping forward I brought us toe to toe and I ran my hands up and down her arms. "Do you, ah... need a hug?"

She looked up at me and laughed. "Sure." Without lifting her arms to hug back she fell against my chest. I was hit by that soft floral scent I couldn't place. It was sweet and subtle, and far too enticing. Shaking my head, I forced my mind back to where it was supposed to be. "Why are you so worried about getting this dog?"

She sniffled, took a deep breath and whispered, "I just need someone in my life who is in my corner."

At her admission I felt something sinking in my gut. As if I was taking something she desperately wanted away from her. The feeling that I was not someone she considered to be in her corner stung. After everything I'd done for her I was hurt that she would say such a thing. Lashing out at her in annoyance was on the tip of my tongue.

"I'm sorry," she said shaking her head causing curls to fall and frame her face. "My dad called this morning.." she stopped, shook her head again and pasted on the fakest smile I'd ever seen. "I'll figure it out." She turned to the door.

"Hold the fuck on." I ran a hand through my hair tugging at the tips. My chest ached at the way she was trying to pretend she was fine, the way she stopped herself from speaking about her father, and most of all the way she thought she was alone. That no one was in her corner. And fuck if I knew why, but I wanted to be in her corner.

She stopped walking but didn't turn back. "Let me finish getting ready for the day and we can figure out this doggy door. I can install it while you're at work if that's all right with you." Keeping as much annoyance out of my voice as possible I tried to extend her a lifeline.

With her back to me she swiped her hands over her face before turning. My gut clenched knowing she must be wiping away tears. "It's okay, I am just having a rough morning." she scoffed. "A rough month apparently. I shouldn't have come here," her voice cracked on the last word.

Growing annoyed again I took a calming breath. "How are you already having a bad day?" It was hardly eight in the morning.

She let loose a humorless laugh. "My father called me this morning and let me know what a disappointment I am. I've been living here nearly three months, and he only started speaking to me again a few weeks ago. And each time is to tell me what a disappointing child I am, how I make him look bad by not working for him, and how I need to get back together with my ex." With that she started to walk away, shutting the door in my face.

Part of me wanted to chase her, part wanted to say good riddance, but a larger part of me wanted to make that wounded cloudiness leave her eyes. I never wanted it to return. The moment she mentioned her father her entire being shifted into something that caused my stomach to clench.

Ripping the door open I stuck my head out into the cold. "Kennedy!" I barked. "Leave your door unlocked. I'll install the damn dog door."

Her eyes widened but she gave me a barely noticeable nod. "It's at the hardware store ready to be picked up, I already paid for it." The sad, vacant expression broke me just that little bit more. She was a pain in the ass but she wasn't a terrible person and, as she said, she deserved to have someone in her corner.

"Fuck me," I mumbled as I went back into the house. *Why hasn't she picked it up already?* Rubbing the back of my neck I debated calling Mimi to get her opinion. She was always so level headed. But she was likely to say, I needed to get my head out of my ass. *Which may be correct.*

After finishing up my morning routine I made it down to the hardware store. Stimpy bringing me the doggy door I needed and ensuring it had all the appropriate hardware included, I stumbled upon one of the last people I wanted to see this morning.

"Oh, Lincoln," She purred.

The hairs on the back of my neck tried to escape. "Hey." I tried to sidestep her.

"Where have you been?" A pout crossed Charice's face.

I'd known for years she had a thing for me, but she was too pushy and loved to tell everyone everything. Something I was not a fan of. If I wanted all my personal shit out there for the world to see I'd sign up for one of those social media blackholes she used. There was never a moment where she wasn't talking about all of her followers and taking pictures. Always taking selfies.

Before I could open my mouth to reply, Howard's hand was settling on my shoulder and the man started blabbing. "He's been helping out sweet Kennedy with her house." Howard knew how much Charice wanted to be with me and this was the old man's way of saying I was not interested.

"Oh," she sneered, trading the pout for a scowl. "That new annoying little cashier at the grocery store? I saw her this morning."

"Fucking hardware store has one that's more annoying," I mumbled under my breath. Part of me hoped she would hear me.

Charice's face immediately went red. Good.

With a childish growl she turned on her heel almost barreling into a display of primer stacked in a pyramid. Catching herself on a shelf to avoid falling over, she stomped back to what I could only hope was some place where I wouldn't have to see her. But knowing my luck I'd have to go through her checkout line. Fan-fucking-tastic.

"So ah, who is the doggy door for?" Howard asked with mischief gleaming in his eyes. "I know Jax doesn't need one..."

I quirked a brow. "Don't start."

Chapter Fifteen

Kennedy

WITH MY FEET ACHING, I made a beeline to my car. Today was shit. First my dad called trying to force me into what he thought was where my life should be. Lincoln had forgotten about the doggy door and I must have looked like an emotional idiot. And then to top it all off my last customer of the day implied I couldn't count above five. The woman wore a smock, the uniform at the hardware store, and I had no idea where the animosity had come from. It was the second time I'd seen her that day.

The temperature outside was cool ,but not too cold. I tried to calm myself as the chilled air filled my lungs. I could do this. Life was going to be okay. Dropping into my car, I checked my phone. Nothing new from Lincoln. I was finally getting close to someone and my freakout this morning was ruining it.

He said he would take care of the doggy door. But I'd hoped he would let me know when it was all set.

Starting my car, I told myself if he didn't end up doing it I would figure it out on my own. I haven't had anyone I could count on in so long, why start now? As I thought that the image of me with the post hole digger came rushing back. Groaning, I let my head fall against the back of the seat, as I drove home hope filled the hollowness that had taken over my chest that morning. Driving in the snow hadn't been as bad as I'd expected. Lincoln had been so good about helping over the last week. I only hoped he'd come through for me again.

Pulling into my driveway I found not only Lincoln's truck, but my father's sports car in the drive. The hope I'd felt fizzled away at the terrible surprise. Anxiety twisted a knot in my gut at the two men being together. After the call this morning I didn't think my father would want to speak with me any time soon. He was being overly persistent lately and I wasn't sure why. I mean he was able to go a few months without talking to me. Why change now? Heading through the garage and into the house I was met by shouting.

"Oh god," I whispered as I ran through the mudroom and into the kitchen. At the stove was Lincoln who had his glare leveled on my father who was in the dining room. "What's going on?" I asked as my cheeks heated.

"I was explaining to him," my father said as he waved a hand in Lincoln's direction. "That he is not the type of man you should be spending your time with." My father turned his entire body at me and I wanted to cower but I couldn't. Instead, I forced my spine to stiffen- preparing for the argument to ensue. "You should be back home patching things up with Brentley, I don't know what you did to screw up such a good potential marriage but you need to fix it. And," he said nearly shouting the word, "you need to come back to the law firm. Working in some grocery store will not do."

I shook my head. My chin began to tremble. I wanted to yell back at him but the words wouldn't form. I felt like a young girl again. The one that could never do anything right. It didn't matter if I was happy with where I was at. It never would. He wanted me to be him. He wanted me to be Kendall. Tears burned the back of my eyes. A hollowness ached in my chest as if it were going to cave in.

"I think she can make those choices on her own," Lincoln snapped as his hands balled into fists. Whatever he had been cooking he'd moved off the burner and he was now making his way over to me.

I breathed a little lighter, Lincoln gave me strength with his presence. "Dad, Brentley cheated on me."

My father waved it off.

"With his assistant. I'd never be able to trust him again."

"I'm sure it was just some misunderstanding," my father said.

Rage was filling me like lava, I was ready to blow. "Oh, you're probably right. When I walked into his office to have lunch with him one day and found her sitting on his desk with her legs spread wide. His face probably fell into her vagina." I nodded as the anger boiled over. "Yeah, now that I say it out loud it is obvious he just dropped a tic tac and was just picking it back up!"

As I shouted Lincoln nearly burst into laughter, I caught him trying to cover it with a cough. It was likely not the best thing to say to my father but I imagined it got the point across. "Also, I will *not* be returning to work for you. That was your dream for Kendall. We may have been twins but we were vastly different. I have no interest in working for you and you need to learn to accept me as I am. For what I am, the stupid cashier at the grocery store, and your only living family. But until that day comes I'd like for you to leave."

I could feel both Lincoln's and my father's eyes on me as I stormed from the room.

"Where in the hell are you going?" my father demanded.

"Changing from my work clothes. You can see yourself out."

Ripping off my dress pants and polo shirt I swapped them with yoga pants and a tank top. Midway through pulling my pants off I heard the door open and close, I could only hope it was my father leaving. Wishing that Lincoln hadn't also left, I held my breath as I shuffled back down the hall to the kitchen.

Finding Lincoln setting the table for dinner I released my breath. "Sorry about that." I twisted my hair nervously around one finger.

Lincoln shook his head. "Don't worry about it. I wanted to make you an apology dinner, for yelling at you this morning," he said grimacing. "And for forgetting I had made that promise."

I nodded as my chin began to wobble again. Usually when a man disappointed me or forgot something he made it seem like it was my fault. Lincoln owned his mistake, it almost felt foreign. A lump of shame was building in my throat. "I'm sorry for whatever my father may have said to you."

Lincoln frowned. "Kennedy, he is a grown man. I will not place the blame for any of his prejudices on you. So, please, don't ever apologize for the things others say and do. There are clearly many things the two of you differ on. The fact that he would try to force you into a shitty relationship is probably the worst of what I heard."

Putting my fake smile in place I tried to bring a lightness to the moment. "So what did you make for dinner?"

"Don't do that either."

I faltered and my chin trembled with renewed vigor as I walked into the kitchen to check the pans. Fear coursing through my bloodstream. "Don't do what?"

"Pretend to be happy. Pretend that everything is fine. I told you about all the shit I have been through last night. You don't see me walking around acting like nothing ever happened. I know you are not happy right now and I want you to be real with me." His tone remained calm as he spoke. I wasn't used to it.

I opened my mouth to reply, but lost the words I thought I had. Closing my mouth I gave myself a moment to compose myself. I opened my mouth again, only to falter at the stern look he gave me.

"You keep walking around with your mouth wide open and you're going to have critters thinking it's some kind of cave to inhabit." Clearing his throat he took the lid off one of the pans on the stove and it smelled heavenly. "I made some sriracha chicken with asparagus. I hope you don't mind spice."

"Not at all," I said, still partially dazed. This man, who made no secret about finding me annoying at first. He not only installed the dog door I wanted, helped me build a fence, made me dinner. Now he was encouraging me to talk through the feelings I have always kept in an overflowing box under a pile of falsities and sadness heavy enough to keep the lid closed. It was strange, but the first thought that came to mind was that my therapist would approve.

Snorting, I shook my head as I headed to the table while Lincoln followed me with the pan of food.

"What was that about?"

"Oh, nothing," I said as my cheeks flushed with guilt.

"It was something or you're secretly turning into some kind of barnyard animal. Piglet."

Again I was gaping at him. "I'm sorry, Mr-stick-up-my-ass, did you just make a joke?"

"Don't change the subject," he said with a chuckle.

Fidgeting with my hair, my mind was at war with the idea of talking so freely with him. But then again, he wanted me to be real. Sighing I said, "I was snorting at myself because I was thinking about all the things you've done for me. The fact you tried to stick up for me with my father, the way you've helped me with everything lately. And I thought to myself that this may be a friendship my therapist would approve of." I dropped my eyes to the pan of food now on the center of the table, perfectly centered on one of my silicone oven mitts. "I guess I was just.. I don't know.. Embarrassed for thinking of my therapist first."

"There is nothing wrong with that."

"Thanks."

"I'm serious Kennedy, I don't know if you're embarrassed that you see a therapist, but there is no shame in that."

For the first time in what felt like months I was able to give someone a genuine smile. And there was something more to it. That it was this man that made me feel safe.One who'd gone out of his way for me, to help me with anything I needed.

Taking the lid off the pan, he served me and then himself. It was so simple yet such a kind gesture. I wanted to cry. I'd been with Brentley nearly a year and he, not once, made me dinner. Cooking was beneath him.

"So, do you want to talk about whatever is off between you and your dad?"

The only person I'd ever talked to about everything was paid to listen to me. And for once I wanted to share the burden with someone else. "As you probably heard, I used to have a twin, Kendall. Well we were about ten and she started to be tired and extremely emotional all the time. I thought it was weird and my mother thought it was just her body going through a growth spurt and she needed all the energy and that was why she was having these aggressive mood swings." I shrugged. "Anyway, when it lasted over a week my mom took her to the doctors.

"They drew blood, sent us home and said they would call within the next couple of days. Kendall and I went to school. I don't remember if it was the next day or a few days later, but my mom showed up and only picked up Kendall. No one said anything to me." I pushed the asparagus around on my plate as I spoke. Meeting Lincoln's eyes was impossible at that moment.

"Turns out she had liver cancer." My voice cracked on the last word.

Lincoln reached across the table, his calloused hand closing around mine.

"It was in the end stages, she was always really small so no one noticed too much when she was losing more weight, but by that time it was spreading to other areas of her body."

"Kennedy, I am so sorry to hear this." Lincoln squeezed my fingers.

Swallowing hard I just wanted to finish, "She only lived another few months after the diagnosis. There was nothing really they could do for her. About two weeks later my mother died in a car accident."

"Oh my god, Kennedy." He squeezed my hand again, giving me that courage again.

"The worst part of it was it was a single car accident. Did she fall asleep while driving, or was it was suicide? I almost wonder if I was a daily reminder of what she lost- the fact that she hadn't noticed Kendall's changes."

"Kennedy, no one did."

"I did."

Chapter Sixteen

Lincoln

IF HER STATEMENT WAS meant to shock me, it did. Because it was now my turn to turn my mouth into a venus fly trap. Kennedy pulled her hand out from under mine as if I'd zapped her.

"I think I did anyway. I mean how could I not have noticed." She ran her fingers through her hair looking frazzled.

"Kennedy, you were a child. How could you have noticed when your parents didn't."

She shrugged and looked as if she were shrinking into her body more. What I wanted to be a nice sweet evening, was turning into a disaster. I shouldn't have asked.

"Fuck," I muttered as I was making my way around the small dining table, and pulled the chair next to Kennedy closer to her side. "Come here." I pulled her to my chest. She was small and warm melting into my chest.

"I just wonder if both their deaths were my fault. If I had noticed, maybe I could have saved Kendall and, in turn, my mother."

Shaking my head, my chin brushed the top of her head. "I don't think you're at fault for either. Did your father blame you?" It was the last thing I wanted to consider, but after meeting the man it needed to be asked. Kennedy was at least twenty five so if she'd been living with this guilt for more than half her life, I hated that for her.

"He never said it out loud, but after that he was trying to make me into Kendall. She was always interested in being an attorney like our father. I always wanted to do something where I could be outside. But any profession I came up with was subpar according to my father so I wasn't allowed to pursue it."

I rubbed her back. "I'm sorry for what you've been through." As I said it I was shocked she hadn't brought this all up the night before while I was talking about my losses. It made me respect her just a little bit more. Most of the time when I brought up my parents it was as if it were a competition to see who'd lost more or to prove they knew what I'd been through too.

Without thought I dropped my head and kissed the top of Kennedy's dark, auburn hair. She smelled of lilacs, I finally placed the fragrance. It was a scent I could get used to.

After kissing the top of her head one last time I went back over to my chair, afraid if I stayed there I would be too tempted to kiss her elsewhere. We ate in a comfortable silence.

As we cleaned up the kitchen Kennedy seemed to be hesitant to be next to me. I hoped I hadn't scared her. She fidgeted with her hair and wouldn't meet my eyes.

"Kennedy, are you okay?"

"Yeah, would you consider going with me to pick up the dog?" She asked the question so quickly I wondered if I'd misheard her.

"You want me to go to the shelter with you?"

Her eyes darted to mine and then back to the floor. In that split second I saw the fear of rejection. Threading my hands through her hair I tipped her head back to look up into my eyes. "Is that what you want?"

She nodded.

"Then I'll go with you," I said as I pressed another kiss to her forehead. Lingering for a moment I waited to see if she would tip her head back to bring her lips to mine. When my hands fell from the back of her head, her breath hitched, and then she took a hasty step back.

"I'm going to put my shoes on." Again she avoided my eyes.

Climbing into my truck we made our way down to the shelter. The entire time Kennedy nervously fidgeted in her seat.

"This is going to go fine, you know that right?" I asked, trying to be supportive. One thing I had never been accused of. It only took me a moment to realize I wanted more of this woman. But she was guarded and kept stepping away from me. I was not going to push anymore. For now.

When we reached the large blue building, Kennedy appeared to be frozen. "Kennedy, you need to open the door," I prompted.

She shook her head.

"What do you mean no?" I asked with a chuckle. "You know this is what we've been working toward for weeks right?"

She looked at me then, those bright eyes filled with fear. "I know. But what if they say no?"

"Then we'll take care of whatever needs to be fixed and then we'll come back."

Sliding to the ground I made my way around the truck opening her door. "Come on," I waited for her to get out. "They're going to be closing in forty-five minutes." she was still shaking her head. "I will fireman carry you into that damn building if I have to."

That snapped her out of it. "You wouldn't."

"Try me, I wouldn't mind having my hands on you."

She simultaneously gasped and blushed an adorable shade of pink.

"Don't test me," I all but growled in her ear. That seemed to light the fire under her ass she needed, because barely a second later she was standing on the ground in front of me. "Pitty," I muttered.

Shutting the passenger door, I followed her up the steps to the front door. As we crossed the threshold there was a loud screeching and the next thing I knew there was a furry beast on my chest as Kennedy ducked out of the way of the assailant. A bright orange ball of rage was clinging to the front of my flannel as the demon hissed in my face.

"What the fuck is this thing?" I shouted trying to pry the claws out of the front of my shirt.

A young woman came flying around the corner. Her eyes nearly bulged out of her head. "Oh, biscuits, sorry." she said coming to aid in the removal of the fiery little animal. The harder we pulled the more he tried to dig in his claws.

"Fuck its scratching right through my shirt." I tried to force my chest back to get my skin out of the danger zone. As we struggled with the cat Kennedy leaned against the door shaking. Once the cat was finally removed the girl held the cat to her chest scowling at me as if I'd been the one to attack.

Leveling the girl with a scowl I turned to check on Kennedy, and it was then I realized she was shaking in laughter. I rolled my eyes.

"Are you ready?" I asked, trying not to sound annoyed.

As Kennedy sidled up next to me she whispered, "I didn't realize you were such a pussy magnet." She was bursting with laughter before she even got it all out.

"I'll get you back for that."

She raised her hands as if she were innocent.

Before I could say anything more Lydia came out from the backroom beaming when she turned in Kennedy's direction. "Are you ready to pick up your fur baby?"

Kennedy nodded then looked up to me and when I gave her a small nod, she beamed and we followed Lydia back to where the kennels were. Kennedy's smile was almost enough to make me forget about my near death experience. As we walked I rubbed the spot on my chest where I would likely contract cat scratch fever.

The kennel we stopped by had a medium size dog in a mix of colors. He was cute and looked to be no more than a year old in my extremely uneducated estimation.

"Hi, Tito," Kennedy cooed as she knelt down next to the door.

My brows drew together of their own accord. "Tito? Like Vodka?"

Lydia laughed and nodded. "It was the name he already had when we got him."

"Just from the name he sounds like trouble."

"But he's so cute," Kennedy said from her spot on the floor.

"I will bring you to our meeting room and let you get to know him while I prepare the paperwork."

Kennedy and I made our way to the designated meeting room, then Lydia brought in Tito. The dog ran around the room in a few laps, then stopped at Kennedy's feet as if he knew she was going to be taking him home with her.

"Hi, sweet boy." On the floor again Kennedy pulled his face to hers and kissed his nose. The simple sweet gesture was melting something inside me. I shouldn't get involved with this woman. "Come give him loves, Lincoln."

With a groan I knelt on the floor next to Kennedy and Tito stretched his body as long as it would go. "Is he afraid of men?"

"He is," Lydia said as she came back holding a stack of papers. "We don't know anything about the life he was rescued from but he is terrified of men." She split the pile of papers in two holding one out to Kennedy and one to me.

"I'm not getting a dog." I shook my head at the papers.

Lydia smiled with something I was afraid to ask about. "I know, Sadie told me you were interested in George."

"George?" Kennedy and I asked in unison.

Realization dawned as Lydia's smile grew. "The orange cat that was out front when you got here. I heard he really liked you. Sadie mentioned something about you two being attached."

Kennedy doubled over in laughter as I shot a glare in her direction.

"I don't know what kind of hell fire that cat came out of but I want nothing, and I mean nothing, to do with him."

Before I'd been able to finish speaking Lydia's cackling laugh filled the space around us. I crossed my arms and waited for the women to regain control of themselves. Once they did, Kennedy completed her paperwork to get her alcohol inspired dog. I couldn't deny he was a cute dog.

"Everything looks good, hun. Were you able to get that doggy door installed?"

Kennedy visibly relaxed and I was glad I'd made the time to prioritize her. "Yes, Lincoln put it in today."

"Oh, did he now?" Lydia asked her tone laced with the implied innuendo.

Kennedy's cheeks flushed as she too caught onto Lydia's joke.

Lydia cackled again as she flipped through all of the papers Kennedy had handed back to her. "You going to make it to Zumba this week?"

"Yeah, I think so. As long as this little guy does alright. That's only going to give him two days to adjust," she said, scratching him behind the ear.

"I'm sure Tito will adjust just fine," Lydia said, tapping the papers on the counter. "Okay I just want to go over what we know about him and then we will get you three on your way."

As the ladies went over everything I crouched down to play with the dog, he was still skeptical- especially when he sniffed my chest where the orange demon had been.

Kennedy clipped a lead onto Tito's collar and was ready to bring him out to the truck. When we got back into the main area, George was sitting on the desk just inside the door.

"Is he waiting for another unsuspecting patron to enter?" I asked, staring the beast down. George's tail flicked as if challenging me to say something more about him. The damn thing crouched down like it was preparing to leap at me again. "Someone put that thing in a cage."

Lydia waved me off. "You're so dramatic."

"That beast scratched me earlier, clear through my flannel. I probably need to get a rabies shot or get checked for cat scratch fever."

Kennedy snorted. "I'll check on you throughout the night to make sure you're not foaming at the mouth."

"You two can fuck off."

George hissed at me.

Chapter Seventeen

Kennedy

WITHIN MY FIRST WEEK of owning a dog I'd learned several things. One, dogs get dirty very easily in Vermont, the abundance of mud and the fact that the weather can never quite decide what it wants to do created a mess of the yard and road. Two, he will eat regardless of if he is hungry or not, there seems to be no end to his stomach. I wonder if that is the case with all dogs. Three, commands are not as easily taught as I'd assumed they would be, granted I got an older puppy that was never properly trained. He was not potty, leash, or trained in any other form that I had been able to discern as of yet. Unless he knew commands in only foreign languages I couldn't speak; he didn't listen to anything. The sound of any kind of plastic crinkling is far better at drawing his attention than anything else. I could shout his name until my throat was dry and sore and he would do little more than look my way. Pick up a chip bag from three streets down? That dog would be there faster than a broke man on payday getting to the bank.

So, when it came time for Tito's first bath I was vastly under-prepared. With the bathtub filled with only a couple inches of water I thought I was on solid ground.

"C'mere Tito," I called in my sweetest singsong voice. Hoping beyond all else that he would be comforted by my cooing. The dirty mutt stuck his head over the edge of the tub to look in. "It's not poison, just water Buddy," I said as I tried to help him up over the edge of the tub. He was a mid size dog but he had full size weight.

"Tito, can you just jump into the tub?" I begged.

After struggling nearly five minutes trying to get him into the bath I ran to the kitchen retrieving the bag of dog treats. Using the treats to entice him into the tub I gave him one as he stood with his paws spread wide. One of those non-slip mats needed to be added to my shopping list.

"Come here Tito," I tried to be stern but he cowered and didn't come any closer. The tub being a large jetted tub was proving to be a problem at the moment. I was too short to reach him if he was in the far corner. Which was where he took up residence when it became apparent I would not be putting the cup of water down any time soon.

"Please Buddy, let me just wash you up." I leaned over the edge as far as I could and when I started lathering the soap through the fur around his neck he pulled his head back. Causing me to scream and topple into the bathtub with him which only served to get him wound up and he tried to run, the sudsy water caused him to slip and in turn knocked my leg out from under me, sending me screaming into the dirty water a second time. Luckily the only things hurt were my ass and my pride.

"Tito! You sit now," I said standing and putting my hands on my hips, as if that would tell him how serious I was.

Sighing, I decided I would finish his bath from here. Especially since I was already fully soaked, no sense in getting my floor even more wet.

"You all right?" Lincoln asked, leaning in the doorway causing me to yelp in surprise and my heart to leap into my throat.

"Yeah.. I ah.. Was just giving Tito a bath."

"Uh-huh" Lincoln nodded.

When I felt his gaze pause on my chest I looked down. The cute pastel pink tank top was nearly see through now that it was sopping wet. I was thankful I hadn't yet ditched my bra for the day. The navy lace was very easy to see through the material.

"Do you want to help me?"

"I don't know, it looks like you've got it very well under control."

"Lincoln, please."

"Should I? I stopped into the hardware store today and Howard asked me how George was..."

I laughed as I bent over Tito to soap him up, with Lincoln taking up the dog's focus he was actually standing still. As I pulled my hands away from him my fingers were covered in a thick layer of dog hair. It was as if I were turning into a bear.

Bending over I rinsed my hands, when my hands hit the water, Lincoln groaned from the doorway. And that was what clued me in on the fact that I was also wearing my teeny-tiny sleep shorts.

"All right back there?"

Lincoln scowled as he made his way across the bathroom to the edge of the tub where I'd been before Tito pulled me in.

"Wait, why are you here?" I asked as it sank in that he just appeared in my house. It was a bit disconcerting that I had just accepted his presence.

"I was stopping in to give you those solar lights to go on the posts of the fence that we talked about, but now that I know you were running your mouth about me to Howard when you ordered them I think you owe me... But when I heard you scream I thought you were hurt so I checked the door and it was unlocked." He crossed his arms over his chest again and the way his forearms flexed called my attention. "My eyes are up here."

"Shut up," I mumbled as I turned back to Tito pouring cups of water over him to rinse him off.

Lincoln's chuckle sent a chill down my spine. He extended a hand to me and said, "You get out and get cleaned up, I'll get Tito finished."

"Are you sure," I asked with my hand halfway to his.

"Positive, you must be cold."

He wasn't wrong. "Okay."

I took his hand and stepped onto the mat and then made a hasty escape to my bedroom and ensuite bathroom. Stripping down I took a quick shower to get the persistent wet dog hair off as well as the dirty dog water. While I washed up I kept thinking of the way Lincoln had looked me up and down, and the growl he'd let out. It sent a chill over my body.

Pulling on a pair of sweatpants, tank top, and knotting my hair into a messy bun, I left my room and checked the other bathroom for Lincoln and Tito, finding it empty I went to the living room. I found the two sitting on the floor together as Lincoln continued to wipe him down with a towel. The smile tugging at my lips was tugging at my heart too. There was something about this man, who'd been a total dick in the beginning, that was now so endearing to me.

"Hey," I said from the hall, suddenly feeling awkward and out of place in my own house–in my own skin really. "Do you want to stay and watch a movie?"

"Sure, but then I need to head home and see Jax, he's been inside since four and will need to go out."

"Sounds good," I said, taking the remote off the mantel as Lincoln moved up onto the couch, patting the spot next to him. Dropping where he'd indicated I wasn't able to deny how exhausted I was. The couch felt more comfortable than it ever had.

Curling in next to Lincoln, I loved the way he always smelled of the outdoors and campfires.

I barely made it through the intro before my eyes were too heavy to keep open. I was going to close my eyes for only a moment, just until the intro song faded out.

But when I was jolted awake by Lincoln's sudden movement I sat bolt upright to see the credits were rolling over the screen.

"I am so sorry, I can't believe I fell asleep." I stretched, nearly punching Lincoln in the head.

"Don't worry about it," he said. The kindness I found in his eyes was drawing me nearer. I licked my lips as my gaze dropped to his.

"Kennedy, I want to kiss you."

"Okay," I said, realizing I wanted the same thing.

Lincoln raised one hand, threading his fingers through my hair. The touch sent a cascading ripple of desire through my entire body. I wanted him so badly and I didn't even know if he was a good kisser yet.

As he pulled me to him, he met me halfway. When our lips met I nearly moaned, the anticipation and build up we'd had felt like the longest foreplay I'd ever been through. When his tongue darted out prompting me to deepen the kiss I opened for him.

Our tongues caressed as Lincoln leaned over me, forcing me to lay down on the couch while he settled between my legs. One hand stayed laced through my hair as the other went to my hip. The pleasure he was pulling from me by simply kissing was unbelievable.

His hand trailed up my hip, under my shirt. I wished I'd skipped the bra. This was the last thing I'd expected to have happen and I was wearing a stupid sports bra. Nothing like a prison for my boobs.

"Kennedy, I want you." He ground his erection against me and I tipped my hips up to meet him. Wanting him in all the same way.

The only issue was being able to let the words pass my lips. Lincoln trailed kisses up across my jaw over to my ear. He nibbled at my earlobe as he wrestled one hand under the band of my bra. When his hand cupped my breast I arched against his calloused hand pressing my flesh into his. The scratch from his hands brought my want tumbling from my lips.

"I want this, I want you, Lincoln."

He groaned, pulling his hand back out of my shirt. Stripping the shirt, I felt sexy as his eyes darkened and took in the shape of me. Before I could take anything else off his lips were back on mine with a hunger I wanted to meet–to rival it with my own passion.

"Wrap your legs around me," he demanded and I did as he said.

He lifted us off the couch and walked down the hall, one hand splayed over my ass and the other trailing down my back. I looped my arms around his neck, breathing in his deep woodsy scent again. Reveling in the feeling of our bodies so close.

When we entered my bedroom he placed me down on the pillows then took a step back. He removed his flannel and then his jeans, leaving him in his boxers and a white undershirt. "Are you sure you want to do this?" His voice was deeper than usual.

I nodded.

"No Kennedy, I want to hear you say it again. I want to know if this is really what you want."

"Yes, Lincoln. I want you inside me."

He let loose a growl and dropped the rest of his clothes to the floor. When I reached for the waistband of my pants he shook his head. I frowned in confusion.

"Let me strip you."

A flush crept over every inch of my skin as he leaned over me pulling my pants down over my hips. Leaning forward he kissed the skin as it became exposed and my breath hitched as he kissed my center over my underwear. At least those had been somewhat sexy. The black lace gave peeks at the smooth skin below.

As my pants continued their trail down Lincoln was right there following with kisses. He devoured, yet celebrated, my body and when we lay satisfied my chest almost felt hollow and I was confused by the feeling.

Meeting his eyes I knew what it was—love.

Chapter Eighteen

Lincoln

LEAVING KENNEDY THE NIGHT before had been more difficult than I'd anticipated. The sadness in her eyes broke me. I hoped she wouldn't regret our night together. I would check on her in the evening, she had work and then her workout dance night was coming right up. I would make sure to be there for her and help with Tito any way I could. That dog was adorable yet crazy–insane really.

As I stoked the fire making sure everything was going as it should, the sap began to boil. It would take all day to get what I'd collected boiled and ready to be bottled. I could get it onto store shelves by early next week. Spring was in full swing. The days were warm and the nights were cold, just the way I liked them. Jax seemed anxious and didn't want to be in the sugar shack, so after a few hours I brought him back home and then finished up what I could for the day.

It was time for my weekly dinner with Mimi and Howard. I hoped Kennedy would be back home when I came home. Then I could use that as an excuse to stop in to see her. Mostly to make sure she wasn't regretting or freaking out about the night before.

But when I was driving down the hill I saw both Kennedy's car and an unfamiliar one in the drive. Something heavy and uncomfortable sank into the pit of my stomach. Tito was outside and clearly trying to get back in through the doggy door but it wouldn't open as the dog nudged it with his nose.

With only a few seconds to think I pulled into the drive.

The garage door was open so I went in the same way I'd done many times before. Reaching the door to the entry way I paused when I heard raised voices. A man's voice.

It had my hackles rising on instinct. Something was wrong. The door was ajar and I slipped in, careful not to move it too much and alert the man to my entrance. The element of surprise would be on my side if I had any say in the matter.

"You are going to listen to me right fucking now Kennedy," the man barked. It wasn't her father, the voices don't match.

I ripped my phone from my pocket and started recording.

"This ring I spent nearly five thousand dollars on is going to go back on that finger, you're going to get rid of that damn mutt, *and* you're going to move back into the house. Everyone will be told this was all a simple misunderstanding. I've given you a couple months to cool off."

Kennedy's silence festered in my gut. Why wasn't she being the sassy spitfire I was used to? Creeping through the entry to the kitchen I didn't see either of them.

"What did you just say?"

"I said no," Kennedy's voice was shaky but resolute.

"Listen to me you little bitch. I worked too damn hard to get on the partner's good side, including your father. So if I have your snobby little ass on my arm, they are more likely to promote me because of who your father is."

Searing hot indignation coursed through me at the way this man wanted to use her. This must be Brentley. I leaned my phone up on the table pointing into the living room.

"I won't Brentley. I can't be with someone I don't trust."

The man was towering over her. He wasn't as tall as me, but the way he was crowding her was certainly making her uncomfortable.

"I don't fucking care if you trust me. What I do care about is the fact that you're acting like a child. You think your dad never cheated on your mom?" The man made another scoffing sound. "You're more pathetic than I ever thought. The only thing I need from you is for you to come back, until I get promoted, then I don't care if you screw half the state and stretch your dirty cunt out even more."

Kennedy flinched at his words. This man was disgusting and I'd heard enough. My next steps were intentionally loud. Kennedy stood on her toes, hope flashed in her eyes when she saw me and I hated myself for letting this ass say anything like that to her.

"Kennedy, do you want this man in your house?" I straightened my spine showing not only my height but the fact that I could easily pound this dickwad into the ground.

"No."

"Ask him nicely to leave," I smiled in the prick's direction. "If he doesn't, I will be more than happy to escort him out."

Kennedy threw me a mutinous look but followed my example and straightened her spine, stepping away from the wall she encroached into his space. "Brentley, I want you to leave, now."

I wanted to smile at her defiance and how her voice no longer wobbled.

Brentley's jaw ticked as he looked between the two of us.

"This isn't over, you agreed to be my wife. I will have what I want. Try not to get any STD's before you come to your senses."

"Well Brentley," I said his name with intense distaste. "I think it would be in your best interest to never come back. That phone there..." I pointed to my camera directed right at us. "Has been recording this entire time. So, unless you want this video shared with *all* the partners, I suggest you figure out how to treat women and, unless Kennedy requests it, never return."

Brentley's face burned with rage, as he stepped closer to me I clenched my fist. Brentley's gaze darted down.

The bastard smirked. "Hit me, I dare you. I will be able to end everything you love like that." He snapped his fingers in my face. I didn't blink.

"I believe the homeowner has asked you to leave, this is your last chance to walk out of here of your own free will."

"You threatening me, you fucking redneck?"

"Nope," I said, rocking back and forth from heels to toes. "Just providing you with an added option." As I spoke I rolled my shoulders as if stretching.

Brentley looked at Kennedy one more time, but she shot him a glare. Then he stomped out of the house and promptly slammed the door. The moment the door shut Kennedy's shoulders sank.

"Thanks," she said, rubbing her bicep.

I stepped closer, taking her in my arms. "Did he touch you?"

"No," she whispered.

I was thankful I didn't have to go and try to murder a lawyer. That would certainly make things a bit messy.

"What was all that about?" I heard enough to have a good idea about what I walked in on but wanted to hear Kennedy's side of things.

"You remember when my dad was here and wanted me to give Brentley," she spat his name as if it pained her to let his name pass her lips. "Another chance. When he was first hired I was working as my father's paralegal. Brentley was hired right after law school, and he was at the firm for a couple of months. And then he started pursuing me. I thought he really liked me." She let out a huff as if she was insane for thinking such a thing. "We started seeing each other and after a few months he proposed. It was such a whirlwind. I thought he was just so overcome by our connection." Kennedy shook her head causing a few tendrils of hair to fall from the messy bun. "I'm so stupid."

"We all make mistakes, Kennedy. Just because you believed the good in someone doesn't make you stupid."

"Sure feels that way."

"I know baby, come here." I pulled her in for a hug and was met with that same faint scent of lilacs. "I am heading to Howard's for dinner, why don't you come with me."

She wiped at her cheek. "I don't want to impose, I know his wife is sick."

"Ha, you don't know Mimi, you think Howard likes to make me squirm? He's got nothing on Mimi, so if she gets to finally meet you for real, she will be over the moon."

Kennedy smirked. "Did you really record that?" She cringed.

I rubbed my hand over the back of my neck. "I did."

Her cheeks flushed as she nodded.

"When I heard you guys fighting I started to record in case he did something stupid. We will keep it to make sure he goes away."

That seemed to make her brighten. A loud bark pulled us away from one another. "Oh, Tito." Kennedy ran to the front door and flipped the lock on the doggy door. "Brentley hates dogs and locked the door before I could stop him." Her head dipped as her cheeks flushed.

"It's okay, he can come. I used to take Jax with me when he was younger, they loved to see him. Go get ready." I gave her a playful pat on the ass to get her moving.

When I checked my phone I was relieved to see the counter still ticking. Smirking, I shut off the recording and tucked it back into my pocket. If I could get Howard alone I'd get his opinion.

Squatting to the floor I pulled Tito into a bear hug ruffling the fur on his head. "You like it here?" His tail wagged harder and he did a few random circles and then came back to me for more pets.

Kennedy came out in a pair of jeans and a tank top that should have been illegal. It showed a sliver of skin on her stomach and I wanted to trace the line.

Clearing my throat I asked, "You do know it's early spring right?"

Kennedy jutted out one hip and glared at me. "I have a cardigan in the entryway."

I smirked, happy my usual sassy Kennedy was back in full force. "You should have gotten a chihuahua."

"What? Why?"

"I just have a feeling that is your spirit animal. Small and full of piss and vinegar."

"And here I was thinking you thought of me as a pig." Kennedy let out a loud laugh tipping her head back. The way her neck was exposed was calling to me. The urge to trail kisses from her ear down her neck was almost too much.

"We need to go before I change my mind and strip you out of that kid's size tank top."

"It's called a crop top you old geezer, plus I'm wearing high waisted jeans"

I chuckled. "How old do you think I am?"

She paused, tipping her head to the side as she knelt down to hook Tito's lead to his harness. "At least thirty-eight."

I clutched my chest in mock pain. "I am barely thirty-three."

"Hmm," She made a face as if she were confused. "Must be all the white hairs."

"I don't have white hair."

Kennedy just shrugged while walking away with Tito behind her.

I ran a hand through my hair, as if the potential white hairs would feel different than the rest.

We arrived at Howard's and Mimi's just as dinner was being placed on the table.

"Hey, sorry I'm late, I brought a friend." I introduced Kennedy and, as expected, Mimi nearly tripped over herself trying to welcome Kennedy to their house, saying if she'd known Kennedy was also coming she'd have bought something special for dessert.

"Hey, why does a stranger coming to dinner mean special desserts?"

Mimi, placed a hand on her thinning hip. I tried to ignore the way her weight loss hit me. "In all the years you've been coming to weekly dinners you've never brought a woman with you."

My mouth dropped open. Surely that was wrong. But as I stood there gaping like a clown at a mini golf course I couldn't dispute it.

"Told ya," Howard said from his spot on the floor with Tito. The minute they'd come through the door he claimed the dog as his own. "Lincoln spends all his free time helping Miss Kennedy here."

"Just with the dog stuff."

"I heard you're getting a cat." Mimi said innocently, as Howard snorted and Kennedy giggled.

"For fucks sake."

Chapter Nineteen

Kennedy

DINNER THE NIGHT BEFORE had been a blast. I was disappointed I missed out on the girls night of working out but Lincoln not only saved me from my ex; but also from an evening of overthinking and turmoil. If I'd known the number of times the couple was going to be able to make Lincoln blush, I would have made sure we'd arrived sooner.

Tito did his best in my estimation. No accidents in their house–thank gosh. But he did almost knock down a chair. Which was caught by Lincoln's impressive reflexes. Now it was time to enjoy a day off and relax. It was beginning to snow and Tito was outside. I wanted to give him a few minutes to stretch his legs before calling him to come inside.

"Tito, come on buddy. I don't want you soaking wet," I called out the door. But as I looked around the fenced in yard there was no dog to be seen. The only thing I could see other than the freshly fallen snow was a pile of dirt at the edge of the fence.

"No, no, no," I chanted as I ran down the front steps in fuzzy slippers. "Tito!"

When nothing but silence filled my ears I cursed. Running back inside I tugged on my boots, grabbed a hoodie from by the door and raced outside. Rounding the fence where Tito had dug his hole, I found that most of his paw prints had already been covered.

"Damn it Tito where are you," I mumbled as my next step had snow filling my left boot. Soaking my foot. "Tito!" I shouted trudging into the woods where my property met Lincoln's. The snow seemed to be muffling all the sounds around me. This was likely what it would feel like living in a snow globe. I could handle the cold, so long as I didn't have wardrobe malfunctions or could hide inside drinking tea and watching movies. Wandering through the woods on a chilly spring morning was not what I pictured dog ownership would bring.

"Tito!" My throat was quickly beginning to ache from shouting and the frigid bite of the air. Just as I was about to go back down the wooded hill I heard him whining. I called to him again racing in the direction of the whine. Between several trees I found the little mutt tangled in what looked like blue hoses.

Realization dawned.

"Oh Tito." I bit my bottom lip. "I need to go find Lincoln, buddy," I said, pressing a kiss to the top of the pain in the ass's head.

Downhill in the snow was more difficult than I anticipated, especially since now both boots were filled with snow and my feet were achingly cold. The feeling in my toes was nearly non-existent.

Since I was already in the woods, running up to Lincoln's house would likely be the fastest option. As I raced up the road I saw smoke swirling out of the sugar house chimney.

"Lincoln?"

As if he were already on his way out the door it swung open.

The moment a slow smirk spread across his lips there was a snow flurry in my middle. This man was quickly becoming everything to me, which was more terrifying than I wanted to admit. "What's up?" he asked, furrowing his brows at me. It was then I remembered, in my haste to find Tito I didn't change out of my itty bitty spandex shorts. At least I remembered a hoodie.

"Tito dug out of his fence."

"Shit really, where have you looked for him?"

"Well, I found him, that's why I came to find you."

Lincoln's frown deepened.

"He's tangled in your sap lines in the woods. I didn't want to just cut the lines but both ends were still attached to a bunch of other stuff."

"Damn, where?"

I was filled with an uncomfortable fear. I only hoped this wouldn't ruin whatever was forming between us. "There." I pointed in an approximation of where in the woods we would find the dog.

Lincoln took off and I struggled to keep up with his inhuman pace. By the time we got to Tito he was even more tangled than when I'd left him. He now had himself and the hoses wrapped around a small pine tree. Lincoln pulled a knife from his hip and with a couple quick swipes he released the dog from his entanglement. Once released Tito started licking and attacking Lincoln's face with so much fervor I feared he was going to knock Lincoln down the hill again.

"Tito," Lincoln snapped and the dog stopped his barrage of kisses and dropped his head. "That was naughty, you need to go back home." Lincoln scowled at the dog and by some twisted miracle Tito started ambling down the hill back to the house.

"How did you do that?"

"It's called knowing how to speak to a dog so they know what you want from them. You need to figure this shit out Kennedy."

The way he snapped at me had me reeling back in surprise. "I... I'm sorry," I choked out, taking a step back from him.

"Fuck, Kennedy. I'm sorry."

I shook my head and took another step back. "I'll put Tito back in the house and then help you fix this." I gestured at the tangle of blue plastic still wrapped around the tree. "Then we'll leave you be."

Lincoln scrubbed a hand down over his face, but didn't say anything more as I made my way down the hill. The snow had luckily lightened up and Tito continued his way straight to the house. He knew he was in trouble and it broke my heart to see the way he hung his head. Once inside I locked the doggy door, put on sweatpants, and pulled on a dry pair of socks and boots.

When I got back to Lincoln's sugar shack he was there collecting buckets and what looked like they could be pegs.

"I will help you put up the buckets, and help you collect the sap each morning." Keeping the hurt out of my voice I tried to remain as strong as I could.

Lincoln didn't say anything, just gave me a look that said he didn't think I was up for the task. I would prove him wrong.

"What do you want me to do?"

"Nothing."

"I'm here to help."

Lincoln shook his head.

"Damn it, Lincoln," I snapped, advancing on him in the small space. The sugar shack was not built to accommodate many people and Lincoln's size left little room for anyone else. "Do you have any idea how it feels to beg for a person's attention? Someone who is supposed to love you? Hmmm?" Our toes were nearly touching at this point. I was not backing down. "You stand there trying to make me feel like a fool through everything. I have already dealt with two people doing that to me, and it broke me. It broke me," I said, my voice cracking.

"Kennedy," Lincoln began reaching for my cheek. I slapped his hand away.

"No, listen to me. I have been made to feel so insignificant that I actually began questioning whether or not my life was worth living. I was bawling my eyes out one night and he came into the bathroom, seeing me on the floor breaking apart. He asked me what the hell my problem was and told me to get my shit together."

Lincoln's expression shifted, stiffened. "Who?"

My breathing accelerated as if identifying would cause me to deflate—to cave in on myself. Filling my lungs with one more deep breath tears fogging my gaze. "My father. I spent my entire childhood chasing him around trying to get his approval. After Kendall's death, and then my mother's, he buried himself in work. He was already an attorney but then he started his own firm. The time he should have been spending with me was instead spent promoting his business. He always said that it was because he needed to pay for me and all the shit I needed. That I needed to stop being selfish.

"Then I started dating that asshole you met the other day. And he did it all to me all over again. I did everything I could to be a good girlfriend, good fiance, but nothing I did was enough. He made that painfully obvious when I caught him cheating on me."

Lincoln took a deep breath.

I was shaking.

When he looked like he was about to speak, I put my hand up. "Please just let me finish."

He nodded.

"I spend so much of my life trying to not be selfish, trying to make sure I could gain all the people around me's approval. After a while, and lots of therapy, I realized I wasn't the selfish one. They were, they were putting their wants entirely above me, which isn't always bad; everyone needs to prioritize them-selves. But it left me lonely."

My gaze dropped to the old boards of the floor.

"I can understand that." Lincoln reached out, pushing his fingers up into my hair and pulling me to his chest. "I'm sorry I snapped at you, it's a lot of work for me to now go out and have to put up buckets. I don't have any line left and I know this late in the season the hardware store won't be getting any extra supplies in. I am sorry I took that frustration out on you." Bringing his other hand to the other side of my head he cradled my face. "And I don't think you're a bad dog mom. I know the way what I just said would affect you, and I shouldn't have said it." He placed a gentle kiss on my forehead. "I am still new to this whole connecting with other people thing. Mimi and Howard are all I've had for a long time."

I nodded. "I feel like I haven't had any real friends until I came here."

"What do you mean?"

"The way you helped me with the fence when you thought I was a total idiot"

"Whoa whoa whoa, I never thought you were an idiot." He chuckled. "I took one look at you when you moved in and knew you were the type of woman I would want to get to know and probably seduce," he said almost as if it was an afterthought. "I didn't want to get too involved with you when you first moved here. You had trouble written all over that sexy ass and I didn't want to tempt myself. So if you hated me, then I wouldn't have to worry."

I let my forehead fall against his chest. His large hands rubbed up and down my back and I was even more terrified about my feelings for this man. I lost my temper and instead of shouting over me, like I was used to, he let me say my piece.

"It's hard for me, because the last woman I was with did nothing but take from me. She expected me to do everything for her. So when at first it felt like you were just trying to take from me I got frustrated thinking you were just like her."

I shook my head.

"I know you're not like that." He pressed a kiss to my head and held me close. "You helped me when I fell down the hill, even though it was your fault."

I scoffed.

"But you've also wanted to be there every step of the way, working on projects with me. Even now, you're offering to trudge through the snow to fix what your dog destroyed."

We stood quietly holding each other for a while.

"Shall we go hang up some buckets?"

"You really want to help?" he asked, not taking his hands from me as I looked up at him.

"Yes," I whispered and then his lips were on mine. Pulling a moan from me as he tried to pull our bodies impossibly closer.

"Fuck me, Kennedy."

"We can arrange that," I said with a wink as I took the buckets from where Lincoln had dropped them during our argument.

He shook his head and a smile passed his lips.

"Deal," Making his way out the door he dropped the taps in his pocket. "After I see your drilling skills."

Before I could take a step out into the cold, my phone began to ring. It was rare someone called me and typically the only person to call me was my father. That thought had rocks sinking to the lowest pit of my stomach. Checking the display, I was disappointed to be correct.

"Hello?"

"Kennedy, what is this I heard about Brentley showing up at your house threatening you?"

It was a good thing I wasn't walking because a, my father sounded concerned *about me,* and he sounded more than a little pissed off. "Yes, he did. He ambushed me at my house yesterday."

My father huffed on the other end of the line. "That's what Walter heard." he seemed to be talking to himself so I waited. "Walter has an old friend who went to law school with him, his name is Howard, anyway, Howard called and told him everything. Brentley's been let go."

It felt as if the air had been drop kicked out of my lungs. Both from my father being upset about someone mistreating me, but also the fact that it had taken another man to get him to see reason. I hardly listened as my father said he wanted to try and have a better relationship. It was what I'd always wanted in life. But as I watched Lincoln study me, gauging my reactions, I realized he was the first person since my mother to be there for me.

Epilogue One Year Later - Lincoln

KENNEDY WAS FURIOUS WITH me nearly a year ago now when she found out what I had done. I had known Howard went to law school but I had no idea that he just so happened to go to school with Kennedy's father's partner. That was just a lucky coincidence.

The interference by Howard got Brentley removed from his position and caused Kennedy's father to try and listen to her. Not only about things happening around her but about what she wanted.

I locked up the sugar shack for the season and started heading down the hill to my and Kennedy's house. My house had been turned into a store for all the goods we'd started to make.

As I trudged down the hill I found her sitting on a bench nestled between two lilac trees while Tito raced around the yard after some old leaves from last fall. The reminder of fall of the previous year had a dull ache filling my chest. Mimi had survived longer than expected, but eventually the cancer claimed what I'd hoped to keep.

I lost more in the last year than I thought I was capable of continuing to lose. But somehow, having Kennedy and Tito in my life made it easier to bounce back from those dark days. It was soon after I had finished sugaring last spring Jax had died. It was almost like he was just waiting for the ground to fully thaw. It felt only right to lay him to rest next to the old sugar house. It had been one of his favorite places to be, huddled in close to the wood heat.

And Kennedy.

She continued to surprise me. I smiled as I sat down next to her, and wrapped an arm around her back pulling her closer. She didn't stay at the grocery store long, once spring and summer arrived she wanted to be hands on at the farm. I had always needed help, but she had ideas of her own as well. Growing flowers and herbs was her new passion. Although I would never tell her that I often had to go behind her and adjust some of what she'd done. She was getting better, but some plants she just seemed to want to drown. She used the flowers and herbs in her homemade soap and candles. There are a few other things she's planning to add to the store.

She had really grown in the community. Cherice took several months to realize she wasn't going to break me and Kennedy up. Since Mimi's passing Howard started coming to our house for weekly dinners. He said it was easier for him to travel than for us to. I think there was more to that change, but I wasn't going to push it.

Her father had stayed true to his promise of trying to get to know her better. He finally accepted our relationship and hadn't wasted his breath trying to convince her to move anywhere lately. I for one was thankful for that. Kennedy had really come into her own here, she created events around town that supported so many citizens.

Thinking of all we'd overcome I smiled down at her.

"All done for the season?" she shifted her head on my shoulder, so I turned to press a kiss to the top of her head.

"Yes, we got more than last year."

She scoffed. "That does tend to happen when you tap an extra fifty trees."

I shrugged. "No use letting the trees on your property go to waste.

Kennedy kissed my cheek and stood. She stretched her back and her protruding belly cast me in shadow. "These last four weeks are going to be torture."

I hated seeing her uncomfortable, but this was nothing to what I was going to witness in the delivery room. I had been told I had sympathy symptoms. Had someone told me they were a thing I would have thought they were lying. It wasn't until I was vomiting in one bathroom while Kennedy was in the other that I went to the doctors and found out what the problem was. I had a feeling this would extend to the delivery room too. She already glared at me each time I complained about anything. Since she got pregnant I wasn't allowed to stub a toe without good reason.

I rose and took one of her hands in mine, dang my back hurt-
better keep that to myself. I led her up the front steps to the
house. She headed into the house first as I took a deep breath in
of the fragrant lilacs and then I turned to follow her.

The changes I'd experienced in a year filtered through my
mind. Some terrible, some exactly what I needed. We'd made a
life together, one that would take us wherever our dreams and
hardwork would lead us.

And it was like deja vu.

I stepped in the door, something large and orange flew at my
chest and there was a searing pain in my chest.

"Damn it George!" I shouted as I tried to pry the cat off me,
while I was accosted by Kennedy's infectious cackle.

Acknowledgements

Thank you for choosing my novella to read. This was one was so fun to write. The sass, banter, and ridiculous situations—I loved them all.

I then would like to thank my mother and sisters again for their critical eyes and willingness to help me in this journey. I can say that it is getting easier to people who know me to read my writing. Even though my stories seem to range in their content, I hope they will be ready for all the stories to come and will continue to be in my corner.

I would also like to thank Whitney Gregg from Literary Fairy for her assistance. Her edits and proofreads helped me to create something that I hope will pull you readers in. Her criticisms have helped me to grow as a writer and have given me so much to think about when I work on my future stories. I hope to work with her for a while to come. info@literaryfairy.llc

Last, but certainly not least, I would like to thank my husband for always being by my side. He has helped me to find where I can improve my stories by asking helpful questions about my plots.

I hope you will continue on this publishing journey with me.

About the author

E. Lynn has loved reading since her mother read books to her as a child. Something about being able to get lost in a book took hold of her imagination. It was not until the pandemic, spending long days and weeks at home, did she begin writing. She found a release in letting out the ideas that clogged her mind. As one story swam to the surface others would find their way into the pool of possibilities. With many more novel ideas on the horizon, E. Lynn hopes to pull people in with her own stories of love, loss, and suspense.

She has lived in Vermont her entire life but has enjoyed traveling with her husband. The first of hopefully many trips will be taking place soon, and although she knows she will miss her kids desperately, she is getting more and more excited as the days pass. They hope to do much more traveling when their children are older. So, until the day she can wake up and walk out to the beach each morning she will live vicariously through her characters.

If you have enjoyed this book, please follow E. Lynn on her various social media accounts for more author content.

Facebook: Author E. Lynn

Instagram: @e.lynn.author
TikTok: E.Lynn

Also by E. Lynn

The Depth Series
The Depth of Their Scars
Coming Soon: The Depth of Their Regrets

Thrillers
Roadrunner Motel

Also in the works, a collection of Holiday and Seasonal Romantic Comedies
Spring in My Step
Coming Soon: Bazaar Holiday

www.ingramcontent.com/pod-product-compliance
Lightning Source LLC
Chambersburg PA
CBHW032012170626
46807CB00006B/2767